THE
FLAMBOYANT

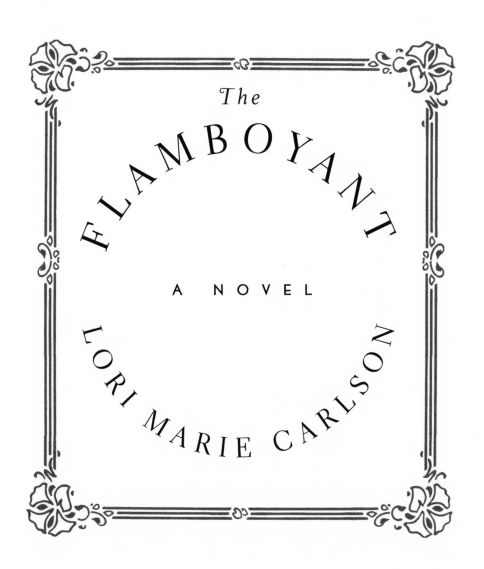

The

FLAMBOYANT

A NOVEL

LORI MARIE CARLSON

HarperCollins*Publishers*

HarperCollins books may be purchased for educational, business, or sales promotional use. For information, please write: Special Markets Department, HarperCollins Publishers Inc., 10 East 53rd Street, New York, NY 10022.

FIRST EDITION
Designed by Joseph Rutt
Printed on acid-free paper

Library of Congress Cataloging-in-Publication Data

Carlson, Lori M.
    The flamboyant : a novel / Lori Marie Carlson.
        p.   cm.
    ISBN 0-06-621068-2 (acid-free paper)
    1. Women air pilots—Fiction.   2. Inheritance and succession—Fiction.   3. Chautauqua (N.Y.)—Fiction.   4. Puerto Rico—Fiction.

PS3553.A73254 F57 2002
813'.54—dc21

                                                    2002020701

02 03 04 05 06 WB/RRD 10 9 8 7 6 5 4 3 2 1

For Oscar Hijuelos, my husband,
and for my father, Robert Vernon Carlson

My flight was done with no expectation of reward, just purely for the love of accomplishment.

—Ruth Law, after having set a new nonstop distance record in 1916, a 590-mile flight from Chicago to Hornell, New York

PROLOGUE

SUMMER 1915

The year in which their daughter Lenora turned fifteen, Louise and Henry Demarest sold their home in Jamestown, New York, and relocated to a sleepy village on Chautauqua Lake. The languid days of summer had seemed to them an ideal time to make the move, as they wanted no disruption in Lenora's schooling.

Jamestown's yarn and woolen mills, furniture factories and decorating workshops, electric lighting company, and water plant were situated along the low, narrow banks of the River Chadakoin, a gentle tributary that wended its way through the city center and met the lake's outlet. And while the prosperous town had maintained its beauty, despite its industrial character—the elm- and oak-lined streets of Dutch-red brick, gracious homes and rolling hills—Louise and Henry had thought it more desirable to live in the countryside, where the air was sweet with hay, the scenery more pleasing to behold. Their decision to move also had been influenced by Henry's keen desire to be closer to Chautauqua Institution. He had been an active participant in its colloquiums for many years.

They purchased a sprawling lakefront estate called Driftwood, a property of several acres in the little township of Ellery. Approximately three miles from Jamestown's city limits, and easily accessible by road and trolley, as well as by a steamboat fleet that serviced lakeside villages, their new three-story clapboard house stood in the shade of towering hickory trees, old sugar maples, and a "spinney," as their English real estate agent had described it, of aromatic firs and pine. Painted the palest cream, and of a grand design, the Driftwood house was spacious, with high-ceilinged rooms, tall windows, and a large front porch that looked out onto the water.

Greenery and wildflowers, Queen Anne's lace and buttercups, stretching as far as the eye could see lent a pleasing touch of wildness to the region's tidy dairy farms and orchards. The area was also abundant with roadside fruit stands, quaint maple syrup shops, and board-and-batten cottages, the latter of which reminded the county's many Swedish immigrants of their ancestral land.

Being sociably inclined, the Demarests began to host small gatherings in their attractive home for old friends as well as new acquaintances—mainly delighted tourists who were vacationing at the Hotel Lenhart and the Browning Hotel, located in the nearby village of Bemus Point. The couple particularly liked the company of progressive-minded scholars, Dr. Arthur Bestor among them, who resided at Chautauqua Institution in the summer.

For decades, ever since its founding in 1874, celebrated theologians, artists, scientists, foreign dignitaries, even presidents of the nation—beginning with Ulysses S. Grant—had come to spend a few days or weeks at Chautauqua's splendid cultural retreat. They might give a speech in the Grecian-styled Hall of Philosophy about the future of the Colossus or amble down to Miller Park to take a cooling swim. Some would discuss Methodist doctrine over coffee and rhubarb pie à la mode at the imposing Athenaeum Hotel. The hotel's management could even boast that it was among the first hostelries in the country with electric lights. This convenience was owing to Mr. Thomas Alva Edison, who had visited ca. 1881, married Mina Miller, daughter of Chautauqua's cofounder, and had built a pretty vacation house on the wooded grounds.

Henry Demarest, a physician of imposing stature, bespectacled and professorial in manner, was as much at ease in settings of debate and philosophical exchange as he was in the halls of the local hospital. Open-minded, forward thinking, his was a nature that embraced opportunities to learn about as many disciplines as possible, whether scientific, literary, artistic, or political. And given Chautauqua's progressive approach to the sharing of ideas and open expression, the doctor's decision to be closer to the Institution's grounds was greatly welcomed by its directors and distinguished instructors.

Ever the gracious hostess, Louise Demarest, a slight, petite brunette with pale brown eyes, was the perfect companion for her more gregarious husband at their festive soirees. She had a talent for listening to her guests as though her life depended on it, and this trait was complemented by her husband's propensity to engage them in a vigorous exchange of opinion, usually about the ongoing war. For by 1915, already several battles had ravaged Europe.

The roomy dining and sitting area in which these animated gatherings took place was decorated with deep-cushioned chairs and settees in soft gray velvet, wine-red Persian rugs, and works of art. Along the eastern wall of that long room were contiguous French doors that opened on to a garden with vistas of silvery cornfield receding into the distance. It was an inviting view—ah, the sighs of contentment—and, often, after brandy had been served, Louise would encourage her guests to take a stroll around the grounds. Everyone, including Lenora, would wander out onto the lawn, eventually surrendering to the pleasure of sitting on the grass. The scents of wild mint and honeysuckle could easily provoke intoxicating reveries.

Henry Demarest had been more inclined than most of the citizenry in Chautauqua County to research the history of that picturesque region. He knew much about the rich indigenous past of southwestern New York State. "Lake Chautauqua or *Jahdahgwah*, in the language of the Seneca, means 'place from which the fish was taken,'" he might explain to his distinguished company, as he tenderly put his arm around his wife. "According to legend passed on by Peter Wilson, a Cayuga chief, some Seneca were making way from our fresh water lake to another larger body of water when their wooden paddles cut the waves, drawing up a large, striped fish. It was a kind not known: the muskellunge. Later, quickly skimming the surface of the great Lake Erie, they took their catch and threw it back to life and, soon, it multiplied until it swam as thick as a storm against their canoes."

Occasionally, he read aloud from the Iroquois creation story, for he liked its poetry. His deep voice would rise emotionally with the beginning lines: "In the distant past, all the earth was covered by deep water, and the only living things there were water animals. There was no sun, moon, or stars and the watery earth was in darkness." At this, his charmed and slightly boozed listeners might applaud.

Often, the guests at Driftwood talked late into the evening, their silhouettes illuminated by the setting sun; a sunset so dazzling that one of their visitors, a landscape painter from Minneapolis, had been moved to rhapsodize about its "salvific, cochineal shadings." While they held forth, Lenora observed their solemn ways of listening and asking questions. Soon enough, though, she would turn away from them, distracted by the tiny lights that flew around her, dancing on her arms and legs. The fireflies.

On those evenings, an array of nocturnal creatures held Lenora's attention. At dusk, standing beneath her mother's clematis-covered pergola, she was amused by the hummingbirds. She would peer at them from behind a pine tree, intrigued by their fluttered dance, amazed at their tiny magnificence. Nightingales sang in the darkness. Fluty-pitched crickets sounded out. And often she would stand very quietly on the rocky edge of the lake, by the dock, to spy the black-winged bats in frenzied flight.

Unlike the evenings of perfect coolness, given to the entertainment of guests, the afternoons had stretched long and indulgent, presenting opportunities to satisfy various personal interests. Louise might visit with her friends, tend to her garden, or make preserves—sour plum and peach, blackberry and elderberry—while Henry, who collected art books as a hobby, would work in his library, tutoring Lenora.

Father and daughter could pass hours looking at reproductions of beautiful sea goddesses dripping in gold, ancient ships, silver-haired sirens, and resplendent winged beings by painters such as John Melhuish Strudwick, William Waterhouse, and Edward Burne-Jones—an endless spectacular of illusion.

That summer of quiet days and luxurious nights, remembered by Lenora, years later, for its fragile, sweet perfection.

PART ONE

ONE

AUTUMN 1916

SIXTEEN HUNDRED ACRES

*U*ntil her mother's sudden death from pneumonia in the spring of 1916, the notion of upheaval in the thrum of daily life had seemed an impossibility. Until the awful moment when her mother had taken leave of the world, Lenora had not imagined that reality could change so quickly. And she would never—not even with the passing of many years—understand why God, "in all his infinite wisdom" had decided to take her beloved mother away from her on such an ordinary, unprepossessing afternoon in April.

The idea of actually moving away from Driftwood and Chautauqua County to live on a remote island in the Caribbean had seemed just as unlikely to Lenora as moving to the Timbuktu of her storybooks. And although she did have recollections of her parents discussing a sight-seeing trip to Puerto Rico once, she never could have envisioned that one day she would be going with her father alone, to start a new life there.

Later, Lenora remembered that the summer they had moved to the lake, a visitor to Driftwood—a politician from the state of Maryland and loyal supporter of President Wilson—had enthusiastically encouraged Henry and Louise to consider the purchase of Puerto Rican real estate a most prudent investment. "Porto Rico" was, in the congressman's estimation, "a fertile land with splendid products waiting to be marketed to our shores, no customs duty whatsoever, a windfall for the country. One positive outcome of the Spanish-American War and the Treaty of Paris. Fortunes to be made there."

When Lenora, who had been present during that conversation, had asked the congressman why such a war had begun in the first place, he had responded by saying, "Well, my dear, the Spanish-American battle was about our nation coming to the rescue of true patriots. We fought against the tyranny of Spain in our part of the world, in the Americas, more precisely." Demarest, wearing his reading spectacles, had shared a knowing glance with her, as if to say, Daughter, let us talk about this later.

Actually, he had spoken often of the nature of combat to his precocious girl. The well-reported devastations in Europe, the Battle of the Marne, Ypres, the constant news of young boys her age dying, had distressed his child, causing her fitful sleep on many nights. He dearly wished to impart to Lenora a perspective of the world that might help her comprehend the motives for men's violent ways.

And, so, that balmy evening in July, after the Marylander had left their home, Demarest sought to expand upon his views. He explained that there had been, quite naturally, distinct and divergent camps of thought on the matter of '98: the Spanish and the American. Furthermore, within the United States itself, there had been opposing factions tearing at the nation's conscience: those who favored expansionism and those who were stridently against it—the anti-imperialists, as they called themselves. And while Demarest considered himself to be a citizen of unquestionable patriotism and had been a supporter of the separatist campaign in Cuba—"those Spaniards are enslaving those unfortunate people; let them have their freedom!"—he nevertheless tried to take a dispassionate approach in analyzing the incident that was largely responsible for sparking that war. The sinking of the second-class battleship U.S.S. *Maine* on February 15, 1898, in the harbor of Havana, Cuba, during a particularly tense time in Spain–U.S. diplomacy.

"The Spaniards," he began, "believe that something happened in the coal storage, a kind of combustion, and that it led to the ship's destruction. They deny any aggression whatsoever toward our country. And the United States, well, it has been put forth by our papers and members of the President's cabinet and, I might add, not unconvincingly, that the Spaniards used some kind of explosive device to destroy our country's ship. They did not want the United States to aid the Cuban freedom fighters. But, in truth, only time will tell. Most likely, the veracity of such assertions will not be known for years to come."

The death of his adorable, beautiful Louise, his "dove," his "honey bud," had shaken Demarest to depths he hadn't known existed in his being. Suddenly, what had always seemed so glorious to him about Chautauqua County—the dense and resinous pine and fir woods, the steely, cirrus-cloud broken sky, the changing of the seasons—red brushed autumn, followed by the silent snows of winter, fresh spring, and mild summer—was unbearable.

He knew that he would never part with Driftwood, he would keep the property for his daughter's sake; yet, he craved to get away from the house and all its memories of promise.

It seemed to Lenora that in a matter of days, gray days marked by cold rain and miserable November dampness, her father had made up his mind about something that he, initially, had confined to the realm of fantasy: buying an estate of sixteen hundred acres in the Caribbean.

He had been perusing the evening papers and had happened upon a notice of sale in *The Herald*. After reading and rereading the appealing description, he concluded that Puerto Rico might be just the place to start anew. He could try his hand at farming; something he had secretly wished to do for years. And, so, Demarest directed his lawyer to make the necessary arrangements for purchase, and in the course of two weeks, became the owner of prime real estate in the little town of Dorado, twenty miles west of the capital, along the island's northern coast.

Being an only child and a fairly solitary girl who had preferred the company of books to other children, Lenora wasn't particularly against the idea of moving to a foreign land; especially a perpetually sunny one that seemed so colorful, imbued with every shade of green and blue. Her father had given her a clipping of the article that had caught his eye: "Porto Rico's ocean temperature is as warm as August rain, the sand as white as sugar. The breezes always kind." The idea of moving to a place so far away, surrounded by the endless sea, seemed adventurous, even a fun thing to do.

But Chautauqua County, her birthplace and the birthplace of her parents, and Driftwood, in particular—where her mother had found a perfectly congenial ambience—would be a place apart, a setting of commemoration. She would return, she vowed, as often as she could.

TWO

SPRING 1917

THE FOUR-DAY JOURNEY

The details of their four-day journey to San Juan in the spring of 1917 would be lost forever to Lenora in a blur of azure imagery. Aside from a few vague memories of the grandness of the ocean liner, what she would recall with sharpness of the ocean voyage, years later, was the moment that George Hanson stepped into her life.

They had met at dinner in the captain's elegant quarters on the first night of their journey. The tall, sandy-haired aviator who had impressed her father with his relaxed demeanor and quiet manner had intrigued Lenora, too, for reasons that, back then, she couldn't comprehend in their entirety.

He had uttered a few words that would define the way she would imagine her future. "I suppose one could say that I am among the freest individuals on this planet. God, I'm lucky. I fly airplanes. For exhibitions and shows. And I have taught flying at Alfred Moisant's school in Hempstead Plains, New York," he said proudly, when introducing himself. "I own a De Havilland DH-2. A British machine. I'm going down Puerto Rico way to see this Caribbean paradise I've been hearing all about. A little holiday for me." The bouyant cadence of his speech made him seem far younger than his years. As he spoke, Lenora noted the fine wrinkles around his deep-set eyes and the strong arch of his blond eyebrows.

"Lenora," he would begin, pronouncing her name, curiously enough, with the stress on the first syllable, "you just cannot imagine how the world moves, truly, unless you see it from above. From the heavens. I honestly think you should explore the possibility yourself. I discern a restlessness in you, something that could take you to the ruby sky." With that, a slow and broad smile played upon his angular features. "You'd be following in the footsteps of the greats. Harriet Quimby, Blanche Scott. Katherine Stinson started flying right around your age. She was just sixteen."

It was also true that the encounter with George had brought about a mood unfamiliar to her—a bout of melancholia. The notion that her future could be exhilarating, full of events and accomplishment, countered strongly with a conversation she had shared with her mother, just a few weeks before she had died. They had been gardening, preparing flower beds for spring, when Louise had tried rather vigorously to make the point that there was no greater privilege than being a wife and raising a child. And when Lenora, somewhat petulantly, had asked her why, Louise answered in a deliberate manner, "Because the love you give to and receive from your husband and children, alone, is really all that matters in the end." The disappointed expression on her mother's face made her feel ashamed. And remembering the disagreeable exchange, Lenora's eyes filled with tears.

She decided that she liked this George, and maybe even more

than would be appropriate. Already, she had begun to fantasize about the two of them together, walking hand in hand, stealing a kiss.

Every morning, after she had taken breakfast with her father in the ship's light-filled, cherry-paneled dining room, Lenora waited for her new friend on the upper deck. She particularly enjoyed George's stories about the daredevil life. Would she ever forget his account of Ruth Law's flying stunt? "It happened just last year," he explained, moving his right arm in the air, his voice dropping low. "She flew at night around the Statue of Liberty. It was a sight, Lenora, one beautiful display, her wings all lit up in magnesium flares. And the word LIBERTY painted in fluorescence underneath the plane's body." She especially enjoyed his tale about a woman athlete, a diver who had made the headlines. Expressing gentle indignation that Lenora knew nothing of her well-publicized feat, he blurted out, "It was in all the papers, honey." And then he launched into an account of her incredible daring.

"Well, Annetta Lipton is probably the only woman alive who can claim that she disabled a great white shark. With one almighty punch. Oh yes, you may smile. But it is true. Good ol' Annie and her husband, Richard, were diving off the California coast. She was down maybe fourteen feet. Richard was already on the bottom when he suddenly saw the shark coming toward them. Immediately, he signaled to Annetta that the shark was going straight for her thighs. Although she couldn't see it, Annetta curled up tight. And then she kicked way out. Lunging furiously with her shoes. Steel shoes, fifteen-pounders. What do you think happened? She kicked him right in the jaws. That shark lost his teeth."

Distracting tales aside, George's accounts of flying around Long Island in his De Havilland had Lenora spellbound. She thought him to be incredibly courageous. "The most important thing to remember when you're up there"—and he pointed to the sky—"is keeping one eye on the ground for a place to crash land. Engines stall pretty regular. Believe me, many a ham and homespun pilot has been saved by his good eyesight. Near the ocean, the beach will do. Near a farm, a plowed field. And well, if there is nothing better, a country thoroughfare. I have landed in all three, and then some."

He was an effective raconteur, to be sure, but it was his descriptions of floating in the heavens, chasing the northern lights, catching St. Remo's fire on a wing, that had truly made her think she would like to explore the sky road herself, someday. And, as George had said, "The year-round summer weather of Puerto Rico offers ideal flying opportunities."

When it seemed that they would never see land again, at long last, on a cloudy Saturday morning, their ship came into San Juan's sheltered harbor. Ahead of them, rising forth from the earth as if it were a natural splendor, was a large, sprawling fortress, framed by grassy cliffs and rugged beach. "El Morro," whispered George, who was standing inches behind her. She stared at the fortress, imagining other times, ancient days, when men wore coats of shiny silver armor and jousted to the cheering of their lady loves. And she remembered in that instant Don Quixote—the eccentric character in her favorite book—whom she thought to be so terribly chivalrous and courtly.

To the cheering and excited chatter among the passengers, the large ship glided gently into port.

A gleaming light blue car was waiting for the Demarests, who offered George a ride into the old part of town. Though grateful for the offer, he politely declined, claiming he preferred to walk. "After all," he added, as he grabbed his deeply creased leather bag, "the only way to know a city, other than to fly above it, is to tread her paths."

Father and daughter shook their new friend's hand and bid their farewells, but not before George Hanson scribbled down his home address and handed it to Lenora, with a quick pat on the arm for emphasis. "Write to me. Do not forget, now."

Then, whistling an unrecognizable melody, the aviator sauntered down a muddy, carriage-crammed road, turning around every so often to wave good-bye.

IGNACIO

*I*gnacio Portelli, the only son of a wealthy sugar manufacturer in the southern town of San Germán, heard from a cousin living in the capital of San Juan that an American man, a widower by the name of Demarest, and his adolescent daughter had very recently arrived on the island. Ignacio, like many other elite *criollos*, or first-generation Puerto Ricans, was keen to have Americans among them. Spanish rule had proven ineffective and corrupt. No doubt, *los yanquis* would create better opportunities for commerical enterprise. They would open up trade, expand markets for Puerto Rican goods. America was, after all, the future.

He had learned that Demarest was going to try his hand at cultivating grapefruit for export in the town of Dorado. But Ignacio was particularly intrigued by talk of the daughter. She was rumored to be a beauty. And, so, the twenty-three-year-old Puerto Rican landowner decided to write to the newcomers to inquire if he might meet them.

It was not long before he received a reply from the American doctor, inviting him to dine at his estate, known as La Sardinera.

When Ignacio Portelli got off the train at Dorado station, on a rainy Sunday morning, with gifts of *pajuiles* (rich cashew nuggets) and a specialty cheese under one arm, a chauffered car, sent by Demarest, was waiting. Soon, he was riding down a narrow road bounded by coconut palms and flowering trees. Leaves and undergrowth, in shades of emerald and absinthe, shimmered from the downpour.

The dirt approach to the estate was sweeping, a mile-long red-clay lane bordered by hedge and jasmine-scented shrubbery, but the whitewashed concrete mansion was more impressive than he had imagined.

A series of gardens, connected by cement porticos and parallel columns, led to the massive entry of the mansion, which was embellished with a geometric pattern of tiny blue tiles. At the far end of the house, nearest the ocean, two turrets appeared like ladders of lace, so delicately worked was the facade. The architecture, modernist in style, seemed almost too pretty. A confection of sorts. No one but the highly regarded Francisco Porrata Doria, he thought, could have designed the house.

From the moment Ignacio saw Lenora walk toward him, in jodhpurs, black-leather riding boots, and a white silk blouse, he was smitten by her meticulous charm. He discreetly studied her slim figure. He guessed she was sixteen or so; younger than the Puerto Rican society women in his set. Skin tanned to a bronze. Her short, curly blond hair fell freely about her face. But it was her eyes that mostly drew his attention; quite narrow eyes that were the exact color and sparkle as the magnificent necklace of little blue stones she was wearing.

"Señor Portelli," she had begun in a quiet voice, "I am delighted to meet you." Taking his gifts, she brushed her hands against his own and graciously thanked him. "Perhaps, before lunch, you'd like a refreshment, some *parcha*, or if you prefer, a little rum with lime?"

She proceeded to show her handsome guest around, finally introducing him to her father, who was reading in his study. Pleasantries were exchanged and Ignacio and Demarest enjoyed an aperitif on the second-floor terrace while Lenora went to prepare their lunch.

Under the boughs of lavish, purple bougainvillea, the three sat down that afternoon to a simple meal of broiled cod and an omelet. Lenora offered little in the way of conversation. The elder Demarest, however, talked animatedly about his plans for the estate's improvement, finishing his list of things to do with an enthusiastic comment about more planting. "We thought we might add a grove of coconut palms near the house. It seems that both the cosmetic and pharmaceutical industries have need of the oils of the fruit."

After several hours of amiable conversation, Ignacio announced that he had better be on his way as it was getting late. "I have business matters to attend to in San Juan tomorrow." But Demarest would hear none of it until he had taken him on a tour of the grounds, replying, "My friend, you are welcome to spend the night in our home. I will drive you to the capital in the morning."

And so, father, daughter, and guest leisurely toured the plantation on horseback. They passed banana and nutmeg trees, acacias and *robles* and looked above their heads to admire the flaming red canopy of *flamboyán*. When coming upon several mature banyans, Henry jumped down from his horse and walked around them, saying, "Just look at these magnificent trees. Extraordinary, don't you think? They must be several hundred years in age. The trunks seem strangely arthritic, yet defiant of time, and strong." Then, pushing the hair away from his forehead and smiling, he got back on his horse and galloped ahead. Down the lane and to their left were limes. Ignacio pointed out the *higueros*, saying, "The gourds can be used as vessels, even instruments." They stopped before the perfectly laid out grapefruit fields and newly planted orange groves, before finally cantering along an exquisite stretch of beach at sunset. "The locals call this La Sardinera Bay," explained Demarest, "because the sardines here are extraordinarily abundant, or so I am told."

Ignacio, who was politely listening to his host, could not, however, take his eyes off the elder man's daughter. He was completely infatuated with the quiet, golden-haired *americana*.

A FLORENTINE MEDALLION

*T*hose first days after his pleasant encounter with the Demarests, Ignacio found that he could talk to his father of nothing but "the blond American girl." Basilio Portelli, a conservative Spaniard who had lost his wife to influenza when Ignacio had been an infant, held traditional views of romance and, although greatly amused by his son's love-struck state, worried that he had allowed himself to be so conquered by a woman. An *americana* to boot. He repeatedly admonished Ignacio, saying, "Get a grip on your emotions, *hombre*. Remember, a man's head must rule his heart."

Ignacio couldn't quite believe it himself. He had always preferred brown-eyed, dark-featured girls. What was it about Lenora he found so mesmerizing? Certainly, she was not so beautiful as to outshine the fetching Conchita Torres or his godparents' sultry daughter, Alma. She didn't have the fulsome lips of Isabel Velez or the somehow beguiling haughtiness of Esperanza Martín. Was it, perhaps, that Lenora stood out among the others because of her grace. Her ethereal manner?

He decided he must somehow impress *la rubia*. And remembering the necklace she had worn, he began to wonder about the possibility of a jewelry gift.

His father kept a few unusual gems in a safe, some family heirlooms; most exquisite among them a sixteenth-century Florentine medallion. According to an expert jeweler whom Basilio had consulted on a trip to Rome, it was "one of a handful to survive, most likely made by the great Benvenuto Cellini himself."

And so it was that one Monday morning, at the break of dawn, while Ignacio and his father, barely awake, were drinking their coffee, Ignacio broached the subject of the jewel.

"Father," he started, "I wonder if I might present one of the old Italian gems to Lenora Demarest. The medallion, specifically."

Basilio, somewhat taken aback by such an extravagant gesture, raised his eyebrows quizzically. He added two teaspoons full of sugar to his third cup of coffee, paused to take a bite of bread, then answered, "As you very well know, it is a rare piece. You have been acquainted with the young lady all of one day."

The recalcitrant son, not wanting to lose yet another argument to his father, replied, "I think it foolish to keep an ornament of the kind from view. Why should not a lovely woman have the pleasure of wearing such a gem?"

Finding Ignacio's response not entirely unreasonable, and sensing that his son's affections for the American were serious, Basilio reluctantly consented to his son's wishes.

After the two men had fininshed the remainder of their breakfast in silence, Ignacio walked quickly to the library. He unlocked the large black metal safe that held the family's rarest treasures. Before him, on a tray, and just as he remembered, were the medallion's elements of near perfection. The tiny pearls that framed the gold casing. The blue enamel, intensely colored persimmon coral. The tiny figure being pulled by a chariot. The soldier, if he was one—he wasn't sure—and the horses leading him were minuscule sculptures, also enameled. Over the soldier's left shoulder was the prize jewel: a large, square sapphire, showing its cloudy age.

It was out of the question, of course, to articulate the value of the gem, but on the other hand, might he not tell Lenora that it was crafted by a master?

So anxious was Ignacio to give the valuable trinket to her that within days he had arranged for another visit to La Sardinera under the pretext of providing Henry Demarest with a few books of Puerto Rican historical interest.

It was early evening when Ignacio arrived at the estate. Barely two weeks had passed since his first enjoyable meeting with the Americans.

Lenora, noticing that Ignacio was worked up—he was perspiring terribly—took him to the patio and offered him a drink, after which she politely excused herself.

Within minutes, she returned with a tray of olives, almonds, and boiled shrimp. "My father will join us shortly," she explained, as she lit a large candle lantern on a nearby table. "He is finishing some paperwork."

Fortified by a fourth glass of rum, Ignacio took a little case from the inside pocket of his white linen jacket. Just then, Henry Demarest appeared, while conspicuously clearing his throat. Looking out to the ocean, Ignacio placed the box on Lenora's lap, saying in his halting, heavily accented English, "Although I've brought these volumes, here, for your father, I happened to come upon this the other day. A little something for you."

She had felt uncomfortable fussing over Ignacio's gift in the sudden presence of her father, and so she murmured her thanks and put the velvet box on the table beside her.

But the next morning, Lenora closely examined the enameled brooch. The combination of rare jewels, the intricacy and refinement of gold strapwork, the rarity of its form, and its apparent age were stunning. Alone, in the privacy of her bedroom, she stood near the window's light and turned the unusual pin around and around. She had never seen a more intriguing adornment.

AT NIGHT

*D*uring the evenings, after they had shared a simple meal of grilled sardines and rice or a chicken soup, which Lenora struggled to prepare, Demarest retired to his study, usually to read about political developments on the mainland.

Lenora went to the large airy parlor.

She loved to look at the elaborately painted frescoes, which were high on the walls, beneath the ceiling's seam: cameos of the Puerto Rican countryside and images of pineapples, guavas, *guanábanas*. She would open the stained-glass windows to listen to the swelling ocean waves just a few yards away, and the croaking, at intervals, like chimes of the tiny *coquí*.

Then, as was her custom, she settled into an overstuffed chair of pale green silk, a teacup in one hand, a book in the other, and put her feet up on a large leather ottoman. Although her formal studies had ended in New York, Demarest had encouraged his daughter to broaden her mind by reading on her own.

She often read histories, biographies, and books on art, which she would select from her father's library. But she had begun perusing literature on jewelry.

The brooch that Ignacio had given her was so fine in its execution that she had searched, with her father's prompting, for reading material in San Juan to help her identify it properly. Where, for instance, did it come from? And when had it been made?

Finally, in one large book, a kind of survey of the Renaissance, she saw a medallion that looked similar to hers. It was, she learned, an *enseigne*. Probably Florentine, designed by a well-known artist of the time. "An *enseigne*," explained the author, a Scandinavian scholar, "was used initially by men in the sixteenth century as a hat ornament. The underside of a gentleman's cap would be folded slightly up and then the medallion would be affixed to or perhaps sewn on. Usually, these cap badges depicted mythological or biblical figures, enameled and jeweled." He went on to explain that many painters, among them Botticelli, Ghirlandaio, and Luca Della Robbia, had been trained in the workshops of goldsmiths, when jewelry making was considered an art equal to others. So respected was the craft that portraits of the grand patrons of the age showed a keen appreciation for the design of jewels; the depictions of great golden necklaces and ornate earrings, painstakingly detailed.

Lenora's favorite portrait in the tome was of the exquisite Eleonor of Toledo, the wife of Cosimo de' Medici, by Il Bronzino. In her opinion, the *parure* of huge white pearls draped over the black velvet brocade of her dress offered a stunning example of regal simplicity.

The more she read, the greater was her curiosity about the symbolic properties of precious stones. Endowed with powers to allure and beautify, jewels were the quintessential talisman. An integral part of history. Wars had been fought over gems, dynasties forged by them, great adventures and discoveries undertaken in their pursuit.

But, perhaps, most intriguing to her was the jewelry game played by sixteenth-century society. She had learned, to her delight, that personal gems had become so laden with mythological allusions, and so significant a part of fashion, that the men and women who were fortunate enough to wear them passed their spare time guessing at the hidden meaning of each other's extravagant acquisitions.

It was in this manner that she decided her jewelry would act as a private vernacular. A language of remembrance and emotion.

THREE

AUTUMN 1918

MILADY

One afternoon, as Lenora was planting a garden of hibiscus and golden allamanda trumpets—flowers that their kindly foreman, Pepe, had recommended to her—she had looked up absentmindedly, wiping a streak of dirt from her forehead, when she saw a petite, slender girl before her. The pained look on the young woman's face, accentuated by her hollow cheeks and delicate features, had caused Lenora to stand up suddenly, as if called by God Almighty to pay attention to her.

"Muy buenas tardes. Me llamo Milady García," began the girl. She smiled slowly, revealing a mouth of perfectly shaped white teeth. She had dark auburn hair, the lightest brown eyes.

"Señorita Demarest," she continued somewhat hesitantly, "I have come from Mayagüez to look for a job. I can cook, clean, sew. I am a very hard worker. Your foreman told me that you are alone here with your father, and that you have no one to help you in the house. Señor Rodríguez is a good friend of my father's."

Not knowing quite what to do in that moment, Lenora suggested that they enjoy a cup of coffee on the patio. Getting up from the ground and wiping her hands on a towel, she led the way to the house, with Milady walking just a few steps behind.

As the two young women began to converse in Spanish—Lenora often stopping in mid-sentence, trying to remember the meaning of a certain phrase or word—she learned something of Milady's predicament. Apparently, Milady's father had fallen on hard times. The recent San Fermín earthquake had destroyed houses and businesses, as well as many sugarcane fields in the southwestern part of the island, particularly Mayagüez. Virtually everything the García family had owned, most important their small farm, had been demolished.

Lenora's mind began to wander. Ever since they had come to Dorado, Henry Demarest had encouraged his daughter to hire a housekeeper, but she had stubbornly resisted, preferring instead to look after her father and the house on her own. Now, however, an opportunity to please him as well as help this girl presented itself quite clearly. Milady seemed honest and discreet. Someone with whom both she and her father could live comfortably.

Lenora decided to take Milady on a tour of the mansion, the gardens, and the farm to see how she might react to such a large estate.

At each turn of their leisurely stroll, the Puerto Rican girl nodded her approval, staring widely at everything and noting the grandeur around her with "*qué bello, qué lindo.*" The house seemed like a palace from the outside, gleaming white, with added mosaic flourishes, gates, and ornate tiled roof. The flower gardens extended to the beach. Just like a fairy-tale picture.

But before Lenora would accept Milady's hasty gratitude, she insisted on showing her the servant's quarters. Were she to accept an offer of employment with them, Lenora wished to make certain she would feel comfortable in her rooms.

Just steps away from the kitchen, which Milady thought to be the finest she had ever seen—the polished dark wood cabinetry, blue-tiled counters, well-stocked pantry—were small but cozy accommodations: a tiny sitting room and bedroom painted violet. And while Milady had known reasonable comfort before the tragedy of the earthquake, this she realized was a luxury of the kind that she could have hoped for only in her dreams. Milady looked carefully around her, admiring the pale purple, green, and yellow-stained windows and high ceilings and, overcome by such good fortune, nearly got down on her knees to show her thankfulness.

It was concluded, then, without further discussion. That afternoon Milady started her new job as housekeeper to *la familia* Demarest.

DAY

During the day, Lenora occupied herself with studying the Spanish language, running errands for her father in the nearby town proper of Dorado, and helping Milady with odds and ends as well as overseeing whatever improvements were necessary in the house. She was also spending time with their foreman's youngest child, a two-year-old named Rosa.

As Pepe Rodríguez and his family lived in a small home at the entrance to the estate, Lenora saw his family often. Mrs. Rodríguez, delighted that *la señorita Demarest* had taken such a fancy to her youngest child, had made Lenora feel that she could visit as often as she liked.

Rosa, or "Rosita," as she was affectionately called, was so charming, so utterly angelic that Lenora wished to have the child in her arms as often as possible. Her skin smelled of almond essence, and it was just so silky to the touch. Her chubby dimpled hands, her little feet, the toenails of which were impeccably cut; adorable. She could spend hours sitting on a blanket in a shady spot, just watching the toddler roll around making amusing faces as she played with shells and rag dolls. And she couldn't resist combing the small girl's chestnut-colored curls, the tactile task reminding her of how Louise had always combed her own blond ringlets, when Lenora herself had been tiny.

But when she found a moment for herself, she would take a quick walk on the beach. It was on such strolls that she often thought about Ignacio. It had become his habit, to her father's great pleasure, to visit them on Sundays, the two often talking so late into the early morning hours that it was not uncommon for Ignacio to spend the night before returning to his home or traveling further on to the capital.

Although the two men were years apart in age, an easy friendship had developed between them. Demarest trusted Ignacio's counsel and admired his intellect. They also shared an interest in political life and eagerly discussed issues of importance to Puerto Rico's future. As such, their conversations centered often on the passing of the Jones Act. Demarest was certain that the law, which gave Puerto Ricans the right to American citizenship, would only benefit the island. But more and more frequently, Ignacio expressed his frustration with American governance, too. "What does it mean, my friend," he might begin, "to be an unincorporated territory? We apparently belong to but do not comprise a part of the United States. Are we not something undefinable?" He would persist. "Henry, *amigo*, the new governor sent by Washington makes no effort to learn our language, or for that matter, anything about our ways. Sometimes I think, although I admit against my better judgment—especially since my father vigorously supports the view—that we were not so poorly treated by the Spaniards, after all. At least we shared traditions. We shared an attitude toward life," to which, Demarest, although not exactly in agreement, would nod sympathetically.

This weekly ritual, these conversations between the men, had also given Ignacio an opportunity to know Lenora better, and his interest in her, she feared, had grown stronger, that is if his latest gifts—books of verse—were any indication. He was clever; he had inscribed the volumes to "my superb Sunday hosts, Henry and Lenora." But the message was clear enough. The poems by a Nicaraguan named Rubén Darío were embarrasingly erotic. He had even earmarked one page in the latest volume, and when she turned to it and saw the title, "*En tus ojos, un misterio,*" she began to translate the short poem that followed, blushing to her earlobes:

In your eyes, a mystery
on your lips, an inquiry
and I stare at your gaze
in a state of rare ecstasy

The simple but undeniable truth was that what had initially drawn Lenora to Ignacio—his handsome face and elegant manners—no longer were having quite the same effect on her; not since she had started corresponding with her aviator pen pal, George.

Of course, she could not deny Ignacio's charm, but that was not the point. She simply did not wish to entertain a serious courtship—the limitations of it!—with anyone, especially since Hanson's seductive epistles, forty-three to date, had encouraged her to see the sky, air, space itself, as part of her being; her right to freedom and exploration. George Hanson's elaborate descriptions of advancements in air travel, astounding stunts, flying tours, international meets, and aviation competitions had convinced Lenora that more than anything else, she wished to fly.

Now, whenever she looked to the blueness above her, Lenora imagined the day when she would be gliding through clouds, quickly moving from city to city in a flying machine. Doing as she pleased and just when she wanted.

GOOD COMPANY

With the passing of days and then weeks, Lenora found that she enjoyed the company of Milady, whose understated ways lent an air of relaxed informality to La Sardinera. The sweet-natured Puerto Rican was an exigent housekeeper and an inspired cook. Embellishing her meals with aromatic greens and spices, her simple presentations of meat and fish were uncommonly delicious.

Milday's presence in the household also led to more discussion in Spanish. The Spanish language, which Lenora had learned fairly quickly, had gradually calibrated her perception of life. The very structure of the language, the inflection of a question, the repetition of words to create emphasis, the inside-out order of declaration, and the softness of consonants that seemed kindly to the ear had begun to influence the way she interpreted the smallest of things, as well as major decisions. When she said, *buenos días* or *gracias*, instead of good morning or thank you, she felt, somehow, more vibrant, vitalized. There was inherent in the idiom a certain elegance as well as tone of joy. She had noticed, too, that an old person, rich or poor, was an old person to be honored. She liked the way the workers called her father Don Henry just as they referred to their devoted foreman as Don Pepe. She also found the communal aspect of the island appealing. She took great pleasure in saying to a guest, "*Mi casa es su casa,*" or "My house is yours." Even her understanding of time had been altered. It wasn't that she thought less of punctuality; quite the contrary. She seemed to have more hours in the day. Puerto Rican time had a relaxed rhythm of its own, determined by the predictable texture of the twenty-four-hour cycle: light rains in the morning, sun and heat at noon, the coolness of evening.

This evolving transformation of her manner, however, was incomplete; in one distinctive way she clung to something in herself that she perceived to be American—her sense of personal freedom; something that she believed was nearly absent in the Puerto Rican world around her, most especially for women. When she mentioned this to her Spanish tutor, he explained that the island was *"inclinado a los intereses del hombre,"* or masculinely inclined, and gave as an example the fact that perhaps the most significant word in the country, emotionally and idiomatically, was the word for father, *"padre."* "From this singular word," said Señor Rivera, "come many words of import to our society. For example, *patria, patriota, patriotismo, patriotero, patriarca,* and many more."

Sometimes, when Lenora was feeling bored, she and Milady would take excursions in her father's brand-new light blue Packard as a form of entertainment. On one such occasion, a gloomy September afternoon, after rainstorms had been threatening for days, Lenora asked Milady to accompany her on a drive to the town of Isabela to do a little shopping. She had been told that there was an industry of fine lace-makers in that coastal community. She thought they might enjoy the opportunity to meet them.

Just as Lenora was consulting Milady about the correct pronunciation of a poetry line from one of Ignacio's books—both women giggling at the suggestive nature of the verse—they arrived at the outskirts of the town. After Lenora made several wrong turns, driving down lanes and carriage paths overgrown with vegetation, they finally came upon a cluster of weather-worn houses at the end of a road.

The lace-makers, young and old, opened up their homes with such gentility to the two women that Lenora had been inspired to compare them to her mother, whose gracious sense of hospitality had never gone unnoticed by anyone who had stepped into her domain. Some of the women sang as they worked. The elderly women went into their makeshift kitchens to prepare strong black coffee.

Lenora and Milady were treated to tiny cups of creamy rice pudding and crispy chunks of *turrón* nougat while they touched and admired the handiwork of delicate accomplishment, everything from baptismal dresses to pillowcases; all articles hanging on clotheslines, as if just washed and dried in the sun.

Among the items Lenora bought that day were some articles of clothing: a loose patterned camisole, faced with pale yellow silk, for Milady, and a sleeveless nightdress for herself. She also purchased a table runner and matching set of twenty dinner napkins, trimmed in lace of *puntilla* design.

It was on the way back to La Sardinera when Milady noticed that Lenora was wearing what seemed to be a favorite piece of jewelry, a choker whose stones were the color of the sea. The very same necklace she had worn the day Milady had met her in the garden. She was puzzled by the collar's seemingly whimsical appearance on her employer; sometimes as adornment for a white cotton work blouse and slacks, other times for a sleeveless velvet robe. Of course, Milady would not have spoken a word of this to anyone, least of all to Lenora herself.

What she could never have known was that the necklace had been an Easter gift from Lenora's parents. They had presented it inside a small fishbowl filled with one goldfish. The necklace had lain against glistening white sand. On that day an ice storm pelted Chautauqua County, the last winter storm of the year, out-like-a-lion March, before spring. And barely one month later her mother had passed on.

THANKSGIVING AT THE BEACH

A gentle breeze lifted Lenora's poplin blouse as she lay in her new, elaborately woven hammock, yet another gift in a succession of many from Ignacio. For an instant she felt the sensation of goose bumps at her waist. It was quiet except for the agitated surf, the skittish song of one small thrush above her.

For whatever reason, whether it was the time of year or the remnant imagery of an especially evocative daydream, she began thinking about the last Thanksgiving her family had celebrated together. The holiday had been her mother's favorite. Louise had always enjoyed the homey preparations that were, in her estimation, essential to the success of entertaining; not least among them the polishing of silver and pressing of linen. She had also been an artistically inclined hostess. Never was her table without an attractive centerpiece.

Lenora smiled, as she remembered an inventive arrangement of red maple leaves and damp ground pine and silver-painted pine cones, which she had helped her mother make the last year of her life.

On the afternoon before their Thanksgiving dinner, the two of
them had gone for a walk in the woods, near Driftwood, to look for
"strong-colored undergrowth," her mother's way of describing wild
fern, moss, cattails, and greenery. When they had gathered enough to
her mother's satisfaction, they went back to the house and sorted
through their cuttings. "Shading, size, and height are very important," Louise had explained, as she studied Lenora's pile and picked
one tall branch of sage from it. "This goes in the center, darling."
When Lenora had asked about a vase, Louise had walked to the garden and picked up a knotty green gourd. "Together, we can hollow
it out. What do you think?"

All afternoon the two of them had cut and pulled and feathered
the various kinds of evergreen and branch until they had formed a
cornucopia of Chautauqua foliage. Simple and meaningful.

Lenora and Henry had not observed Thanksgiving since Louise's
death, preferring instead to get through the day as best they could
with, perhaps, a lunch of special stew followed by an excursion to San
Juan to see a movie or theatrical production. But as she lay in her
hammock, moved by her memories, she wondered if they shouldn't
try again to celebrate the holiday. Milady's accomplished cookery
combined with the possibility of enjoying an American tradition
with their Puerto Rican friends would be an ideal way to introduce a
little familiarity, a bit of their old life, into their island existence.

When Lenora proposed the idea to her father later that afternoon at tea, he seemed quite pleased by the notion. He, too, had
missed the pleasure of sitting around a beautifully laid table with
good food in the company of interesting friends. And he was starting

to feel as though he might be able to carry on without Louise, if only to be an example of fortitude to his daughter.

After much discussion, they decided on a guest list. Of course, Ignacio would be invited and a few American businessmen who worked in San Juan, among them their associate Jonathan Mansfield. And then there were several Puerto Rican artists and writers whom Demarest had admired but did not know well. Their foreman, his wife Marianela, and their five children. And Lenora could not forget the kindly jeweler in San Juan, a Spaniard named Iglesias, who lent her books on jewelry whenever she stopped by his shop.

With the guidance of Milady, Lenora then decided on a menu. They concocted a five-course feast. For the starter, avocado, simply sliced, sprinkled with lemon, olive oil, salt, and pepper. Next a soup, a light fish soup, served not too hot; just warm enough to let the subtle flavors of *ají* and pineapple, cinnamon, coconut, and shrimp pique their guests' appetite. Although nothing in Lenora's opinion could possibly be as tasty as roast turkey, Milady insisted that barbecued pork would make an excellent substitute. The thought of roasting a whole pig had sounded overwhelming to Lenora, but Milady assured her that a few of the field hands could handle the more demanding aspects of the spitting and roasting. "It is not hard. You will see," she had countered in her most convincing tone of voice, and added, as if to put the matter to rest, "the meat is so sweet and juicy and the skin so crispy golden that you'll want to eat it every day." The fourth dish, Lenora insisted, should be something typically American.

"A simple salad, I think."

"No, no."

"Maybe some green vegetables. Or potatoes. Or stuffing. Stuffing would be my preference."

"And what is stuffing?"

"Bread, *pan, con cebolla,* onion, carrot, sage, *hierbas, un poquito de chorizo,* mixed together with broth and butter, then baked. In America we eat it at Thanksgiving."

"*Bien.* But I cannot make this. Can you?"

"I really don't know. But I can try."

And, finally, they came to the fifth and final course of dessert without argument. "The best thing to do," said Lenora, pointing to a large bowl of ripe papayas and mangoes, "is serve fruit. And maybe milk chocolates and nuts."

ENJOYMENT

As the holiday approached, Lenora and Milady occupied themselves with myriad household chores. They thoroughly cleaned every surface in the house, waxing wood doors and wainscotting, molding, and cabinetry. They scrubbed the richly patterned tile floors. Washed fuschia-tinted crystal goblets (heirlooms from her mother's family) and polished flatware. Lenora also made a centerpiece of coral, shells, and tall white candles, the deep shades of pink and russet working beautifully against the antique beige of what had been her mother's favorite linen tablecloth.

On Thanksgiving Day, the two women worked all morning and

afternoon. Milady had begun her work early. As soon as she had risen, she had supervised Pepe and a few of the farmhands while they prepared an immense suckling pig for roasting in the clearing at the back of the house, under an open-air hut, thatched in straw. Then, she returned to the kitchen to make her soup, as well as various sauces. She cut fruit into chunks and splashed them with rum. She arranged the Spanish chocolates, marzipan, and roasted nuts on various cut-glass plates. Finally, she decanted the wine.

Meanwhile, in the dining room, Lenora was setting the table, using her mother's best china, an English pattern of bees and black-berries, and the napkins that she had bought in Isabela. She added small white flowers to the table arrangement.

When everything was perfectly in place, the silver and sparkling crystal, she stepped back from the table, closed her eyes and opened them, as she had seen her mother often do. She thought the dining room looked every bit as lovely as the dining room at Driftwood.

At six o'clock, exhausted but satisfied with what they had accomplished, each woman went to her respective room to freshen up and dress. Lenora wore her favorite gown, a long silk navy dress with short capped sleeves, worked in braiding and velvet appliqué. As for her jewelry, a recent purchase: a very simple French tiara, so delicately rendered in silver threading and turquoise beads that it could barely be seen beneath her curls.

That festive evening, Demarest, sitting at the head of the table, thoughtfully took in the scene around him. He felt enormously proud of his daughter. She had done a fine job of introducing guests to one another; and he noted that she was exceptionally attentive to them throughout the dinner. He was pleased, too, with the culinary skills of their very pleasant housekeeper. Lenora had chosen well.

He watched his daughter, who was holding Rosa in her lap, more closely. What could that promising, young poet, Palés Matos, be saying to make her laugh so? Ignacio was having a serious conversation with Jonathan Mansfield about the large, aggressive American sugar corporations suddenly appearing on the island. "They're going to run us out of business, Mansfield," complained Ignacio. "My family's company is relatively small. What are we to do?" The elderly Señor Iglesias, a refined-looking gent, in striped gray suit and sporting a handsome gold pocket watch was admiring the centerpiece. Dr. Barbosa was talking animatedly with Ignacio, arguing that Puerto Rico should become a state like any other, while savoring his wine with quick little slurps between pauses. The great José de Diego, his cheeks flushed with emotion, was making his case to the American businessmen about the horrors of colonialism. "We must find a way to exert our independence," he kept repeating. And Pepe was enjoying his food to such an exuberant extent that he was unaware of everyone around him, including his overly animated children who had begun, a bit annoyingly, to pelt each other with bits of greasy pork rind.

After the chocolates had been served, José de Diego stood up slowly and launched into a recitation of "Aguadilla," among his most beloved poems. When he had finished, and all the guests were marveling at the lilt of his delivery—he was, without doubt, the island's greatest orator—wine was poured again. Then, Pepe, who had brought along his guitar, began to play a *danza*. There were *palmas y pitos*, and a sudden reason to dance. Ignacio, quickly getting up from his chair, pulled Lenora to her feet and led her to the parlor.

As Ignacio gently pulled her closer to him, she felt the blood rush to her cheeks. She had never danced in a romantic way before and the feeling of a man's skin underneath her fingertips, the brushing of his thigh against her own, made her feel a bit light-headed.

Demarest observed the young couple in their moment of spontaneous joy. He approved of Ignacio, and should he and Lenora some day marry, he would not object. He closed his eyes. Puerto Rico had brought them many blessings, not least among them these fine people. The work at La Sardinera was going well. Lenora seemed content. And the war in Europe had finally ended; that in itself was reason to rejoice.

FOUR

WINTER 1919

COLOGNE

The letter resting in her hand, the most recent from George, bore an agitation of tone dissimilar to the many other letters he had sent her. And there was something else about it—his neatly written note ended with a challenge: if she was as interested in flying as she had indicated in her correspondence, when was she going to begin? "At some point you have to make the leap from thinking about planes to piloting. And the sooner the better, before you lose heart. Doggone, you have to chase away the hoodoo, kid." The letter also described in exciting detail the most amazing recent event in aviation: the first successful crossing of the Atlantic Ocean by "Putty" Reed, a navy seaplane pilot, and his five-man crew.

Whether she was held back by fear or the habit of spending her leisure time firmly footed on the farm, she had not been able to focus her energies on the undertaking of buying a plane and finding an instructor. Who, for heaven's sake, would solo her? And in Puerto Rico? She could not imagine it. Furthermore, she was slightly disheartened by her father's reaction to taking up the enterprise. "What is this fancy of yours, my dear?"

She never, despite feeling hurt, protested his attitude; she merely smiled when he disagreed with her.

But beyond her father's rebuke, it was his behavior that concerned her of late. It had occurred to her, though she was not sure, that he had been paying more amorous than patronly attention to Milady.

He had never, as far as she could remember, worn a scent before. Now, every morning at breakfast she was aware of his cologne, an air of cloves with licorice. And he had begun to comb his hair differently. In and of themselves these changes, she supposed, would have meant little if they had not been accompanied by his countless inquiries regarding their housekeeper: "Is this Milady's day off?" "Is Milady going to the market this morning?" "Perhaps Milady would like to join us for tea?"

Lenora chose to act as though she hadn't noticed this increased interest in their employee. After much consideration of her father's right to privacy and the close bond that existed between them, she chose to watch what was happening in silence. She was aware that as she got older, she was becoming in this regard much like her mother. She was introspective, prone to long reveries. When something troubled her she preferred to find solutions within herself rather than seek them through an endless series of interactions with others. Silence was golden, it was true; the ability to think through her emotions without having to explain herself.

She thought of the endless confusions, moments of hurt feelings, false contentments, caused by careless speech. So often what one meant to say came out differently, changing situations and relationships instantly, sometimes irrevocably.

What was it about the spoken word that actually diminished the speaker? She knew that many, if not most people, thought differently; that disputes could be settled with words, misunderstandings would be erased with explanations, or even that the most profound human feelings must be declared. But, no, she did not share these views. She believed that conversation in and of itself was poor at getting to the truth.

Whatever was transpiring in her father's heart, whatever his feelings for Milady, at the very least, deserved her quiet respect.

OFF THE KITCHEN

*I*t had been nearly two years since Milady had moved to the *finca Demarest* as she called what she considered to be her magnificent, but temporary, home. Until the moment when she walked into La Sardinera's garden on the first day she had met Lenora, she never would have imagined she might live in such a grand environment. Life in the house of tinted glass and gleaming tiles, stenciled walls, and furnishings went beyond all expectation for a girl from the country.

At night, after all her daily chores had been completed—the meals made, the dishes washed, the patio and terraces swept, and flower beds watered—Milady would return to her sitting room to draw. And while she drew her whimsical pictures of swans and palaces, fountains and flowers, she dwelled on private matters; most often, her family.

She wrote to her parents twice a week, having learned to accept, however difficult, the distance that separated them. But when she thought about the impoverished circumstances under which her mother and father lived, she would weep until she was so tired she could barely muster preparing for bed.

And she was preoccupied by something else; the gentle, yet persistent, flirtations of Henry Demarest.

She had first become aware of her employer's advances just after Thanksgiving that first year with the family. One morning, when she had given him his usual breakfast of scrambled eggs and *chorizo*, toasted bread, and sliced quince confit, instead of merely thanking her, he suggested she sit down and join him and his daughter for coffee. Startled by his offer—she knew her place was in the kitchen—she had glanced at Lenora and judging from the confused expression on her face, politely declined, saying, "Thank you, sir, but I have much to do. *Gracias, de nuevo.*" Then she quickly walked to the swinging latticed door that separated their world from hers.

The situation had not simply slipped away as quickly as she had on that peculiar morning. Rather, Señor Demarest continued to pursue, it seemed, her every move. If Milady was working on the patio and he walked by, not only would he stop to chat but he might also invite her to accompany him on his daily constitutional.

On one such awkward stroll, when she had mentioned that her hobby was sketching, he had replied, "May I come to see a few of your pictures one evening?" She had demurred, but at the same time wondered if she might not like to have his company. He was kind, good-natured, and not so very old as to be a totally unsuitable *pretendiente*.

In the end, though, Milady knew that she must be correct, for if she failed to keep a proper distance from the family, she might well lose her position. It was one thing to be on friendly terms with his daughter, nearly the same age as she, but quite another to engage in private, evening meetings with Señor Demarest. The thought of having to leave the house and, most important, work that enabled her to provide a little income for her family, as well as losing the respect of Pepe—she owed her job to him—simply terrified her.

Yet, at the same time, she could not deny how proud she felt that someone so intelligent, well bred, and wealthy, *un americano protestante*, might be attracted to her, a simple country girl, a Catholic, from Mayagüez.

PART TWO

FIVE

AUTUMN 1923

ALONE AT DRIFTWOOD

$\mathcal{B}$ ecause there was a chill in the air and a heavy frost had blanketed the lawn at Driftwood, Lenora sat wrapped in a woolen shawl on the wide front porch, facing the lake. She watched a lone fisherman guide his rowboat to a spot not far from where the dock would have abruptly ended in the water had it been summertime. And well beyond his small wooden vessel, tooting their imminent arrival at the Greenhurst dock, were two majestic steamboats, the *City of Cincinnati* and the *City of New York*.

No longer did she simply see the lake as blue, the sky as overcast, the gardens as well maintained. No longer did she think of the house as especially grand. Driftwood, the dearest gift she had ever been given, a present from her father on the occasion of her twentieth birthday, had become an alternate home for her, a contrast to Dorado. A once-a-year retreat to revel in the glorious autumnal turning of the leaves. The fall months had always been her favorite.

Chautauqua Lake was a blue less green than turquoise, the sky was steely in mood because it lacked the ocean winds that kept the

Puerto Rican air so transparent, and the gardens, which her mother had designed to please, seemed terribly proper without the wild, lush lines of tropical foliage she had come to favor. The Driftwood architecture was solid, ordinary in comparison to the combination of colored glass and ornate Spanish tiles that adorned their Puerto Rican residence. And, yet, she loved reconnecting with the land of her birthplace, the wellspring of her soul. At her New York home, she cherished the time to think.

This morning she was allowing herself the pleasure of imagining the extraordinary objects described in the book before her. A book by a certain Fritz P. Imbert. So detailed and comprehensive, even academic, was Imbert's summary of famous jewels that it proved to be a kind of bible on the subject. She savored the minutiae and intriguing tales he divulged with unabashed delight.

She considered the torturous example of Elizabeth I, Queen of England, and her beloved Earl of Essex. What might have happened if the ill-fated Essex, accused of treason and locked away, had managed to return to Elizabeth the ring of favor she had given him. Hadn't his sovereign assured him the ring would serve to speak for Essex? That if ever he required her forgiveness, no matter the transgression, he need only send the jewel back to her; the true sign of his loyalty. Surely he would not have been beheaded by order of the lady he loved best had his courier, with the ring upon his person, not mistakenly and tragically delivered it to a countess who gave the ring to Essex's arch-nemesis.

She was intrigued by the text accompanying one black-and-white print of a Spanish queen, Elisabeth de Valois. Imbert pointed out a certain large pearl dangling from her intricately plaited hair. It was, he said, the famed La Peregrina, also known as the Wanderer, considered to be the pearl of Spanish queens. Every regent since the time of Philip II had her portrait painted with it. But not only that. Imbert, in a tone that seemed gleefully conspiratorial, revealed the story of how this pearl had been discovered. In 1550, a slave had come upon the gem in Panama; it had washed up on a beach. Because the pearl was very large, ovoid in shape, the slave upon handing it to his master, a Spanish nobleman, was given with sheer aristocratic gratitude his freedom.

The range and complexity of jewelry-making, described by Imbert, had opened up an unknown world to her. She had always assumed that women's jewels were, simply, rings and bracelets, earrings, pins. But she had come to discover that there had been a wide variety of feminine adornments through the ages. Stomachers, aglets (decoration for the skirt and bodice of a dress) coronals (headbands) and buckles, chatelaines and girdles (to be worn around the waist), corsages, aigrettes (jeweled ribbons for bonnets and hats), and carcanets (for the neck).

She looked up to see a flock of geese fly in formation above the brown-leafed hickory trees, circling again and again, going nowhere, as if to accompany her in this early morning reverie. And, then, a small fawn appeared at the edge of the lake.

She thought about the chores ahead of her. In just three weeks, she would be returning to the island. There were leaves, great endless piles of wet damp sugar maple, oak, and withered willow leaves to be raked; flower beds to bank; discussions with the caretaker of the house, a certain Dr. Bloomberg; meetings with her father's lawyer; and some sundry shopping to be done in Jamestown. There were windows to be washed, linens to be aired and ironed, then packed away. Because she visited just once a year, there was much to do in little time. But Driftwood was her house, and with ownership came pride. The pride of knowing that there was a bit of the world to keep, a bit of safety somewhere, just for her. And this house held precious memories. Each room contained something of her mother's being. Would she ever be able to enter the large, white-tiled kitchen without suddenly smelling the sweet thickness of peach preserves, bubbling on the stove top, or the pungency of freshly snipped chives, the aroma of roasted cornish hen? Would she ever be able to step into the drawing room without remembering her mother in a favorite ivory wool dress, sitting in a gray velvet chair, embroidery in hand?

Lenora got up from the porch swing and, seeing that the lanky fisherman had taken off his cap and nodded to her, waved back, smiling. She walked down the creaky wooden steps to the moss-embedded flagstone path. She examined the gardens in the back. Rust-colored mums fell every which way over little yellow pumpkins. The bird feeders needed repainting.

Glancing at her wristwatch, she realized she had better take a bath and dress. Her lunch date was at noon. And she intended to visit her mother's gravesite on the way.

AN OFFER

*D*riving slowly along Chautauqua Lake in her father's old Ford roadster, past cornfields and long stretches of pitch-shadowed woodland, patches of pine forest, and open marsh, Lenora felt as if she were being held down, bound by the earth. So different from the feeling of openness conveyed by the island's ocean landscape. She had come to adulthood, rather surprisingly in a setting so unlike this brooding land.

She followed the curve of the highway at the lakeside community of Mayville, just short of the city limit, past the train station and the Hotel Houx. The colors of the falling leaves—pigeon blood and topaz, flagrant amber—cut across the sky. It was a typical autumnal day, a day in which to revel in the simple act of breathing. She took great gulps of crisp, cold air.

She had received George Hanson's most recent letter before leaving Dorado for Driftwood—a letter in which he suggested that they meet in a convenient place, close to her Driftwood home. As it happened, his flight plan took him flying near Chautauqua when she would be staying at her New York estate. He was planning to attend an air meet in Buffalo, New York. Would she meet him for lunch in the village of Westfield? He had, he believed, "an interesting offer" for her.

The mysterious tone of George Hanson's letter coupled with the prospect of seeing him again had elicited her enthusiastic reply.

As she dressed that morning, she wondered if she had chosen her attire well. She wished to look especially fetching, but not obviously so. In the end, after having tried on several suits but thinking that each one looked rather formal, she opted for a simple v-neck jersey dress with matching cardigan jacket in evergreen, sleeves tapered to just below the elbow. At the last minute she had on a brimmed cloche in tawny felt with a touch of mink trim.

And, so it was that on that bright afternoon Lenora drove to a small café called Nettie's, across the street from Westfield's much frequented town square. Nettie's was directly opposite a white gazebo, in which, during the summer months, small impromptu bands played to the pleasure of toddlers and their parents and grand-parents, all of them stretched out on flannel blankets, devouring peach and butter pecan ice creams, under the moon.

Lenora entered through the restaurant's front door, nervously touching the tiny gold and emerald four-leaf clover pin on her lapel, and looked around. As she pulled off her kidskin driving gloves, her gaze fell upon him. She noticed he had grown more handsome; his deep-set eyes more intriguingly wrinkled, his eyebrows slightly tinged with gray.

The dashing aviator, dressed in gray woolen pants, cream-colored silk scarf, and worn brown leather jacket, was sitting close to the wall at a table for two. He was studying a map, his elbows resting on the white linen tablecloth. A single pink rosebud in a tiny vase before him. Upon seeing the woman he had first met on the sea years before and now knew solely through her correspondence, he took a deep breath.

She was, aside from the impressive physical flowering that had occurred over the past seven years, somehow changed. She was in command of herself. The way she walked, held her head, intrigued him.

After she sat down, he simply said, "I'd like to take you up today."

IN THE SKY, THE SCENT OF GRAPES

The first impression she had that afternoon of being in the sky was hindered by excitement. She had never been a nervous sort. She had, however, felt throughout her life a choking anticipation whenever she intuited that something especially wonderful was about to happen. And in those instances when she simply could not help herself, in times of heightened happiness, it seemed her entire body was quickly moving, yet still. She felt it in her skin. A kind of prickly sensation, as though the blood that ran in unknowable threads within her was coming to a boil. Then she would feel a catch in her throat.

As they swiftly lifted off the ground in George's gleaming, bronze Curtiss Oriole, his most recent "bird," adjacent to a vast, half-harvested vineyard near the village center, she felt unable to acknowledge that they were flying, as if she were coping with the old, familiar reaction. But once they reached a level altitude, she leaned back in her seat and looked out at the sky. Of course she noted the dusty blue, the bands of light and wash of clouds, but more than anything else she felt a part of infinity. The plenitude of nothing and everything.

For seven years, through sentences that informed, cajoled and inspired her, amused and challenged her, she had come to know and respect this most unusual friend. She appreciated this confident man for what he had chosen to give her: encouragement, the desire for new experience, for understanding that there truly was more than one string to her bow. For his generosity, for caring how she fared in Puerto Rico, for expecting her to excel at what she wished to do. And now, for giving her the sky and all its wonderment—it was, she marveled, possible to taste its purity, to smell the air's invisible veil, scented with the ripened fruit beneath them; the sour-sweet fragrance of Concord grapes.

She looked below her, seeing barns and farmhouses in a red and yellow puzzle, white silos, endless vineyards, orchards—apple, peach, pear, and cherry—fern-thick vales. Rocky gorges, pine-covered hills. And, oh, the lakes, the shimmery Lake Erie and the staid Chautauqua. From the sky this country was a tapestry. A tapestry woven of natural randomness, and hard work, of plowing and planting, preparing, praying, despairing, and hoping. A bountiful land of hamlets and small towns with names like Mayville, Lakewood, Celeron, Westfield, Fredonia, Barcelona, and farther on, Salamanca.

For the first time in her life she thought of farming as a holy dedication. Looking down on the burnished foliage, the rolling, soft countryside she had known since she was a small girl, it occurred to her that this was a land that flourished because of great labor—the faith of good people.

Ahead of her in the front cockpit, George waved his arm and pointed downward. And, so, they followed a gust that, in a long loop, took them slowly through great viscous clouds like large *medusas*, the sounds of cowbells soaring up to them *so clearly*, and down and lower to the place from which they had alighted, back to the grape field of some unknown farmer, back to the tedium of earth.

After they embraced against a flaming maple tree, Lenora trembling from emotion, they said their shy farewells.

In the stinging light of an early winter's afternoon, she knew that she had been changed forever. As she stood still, pulling her jacket around her tightly, she watched as George's plane, Buffalo-bound, flew into the air, that unknowable sea of possibility, waving good-bye and leaving her with an almost unbearable yearning for something she could not identify.

THE WOMEN WHO SOARED

*J*ust one day after George's uneventful air meet in Buffalo, he penned, perhaps, the most earnest letter of his life. He felt certain that if he could sum up in convincing detail the many daring and marvelous exploits of international women pilots, Lenora would have no choice but to finally accept his offer to solo her. He wrote about England's Hilda Hewlett, and "the Cardinal of the Sky" Edith Spencer Kavanaugh, the Americans Blanche Stuart Scott, billed "The Tomboy of the Air," Matilde Moisant, Katherine Stinson and Marjorie Stinson, Bessica Raiche, the Russian Lidia Zvereva. Japan's Tadashi Hyodo, France's Raymonde de Laroche. Hélène Dutrieu of Belgium, known as "the Girl Hawk," the German Melli Beese, Italy's Rosina Ferrario, and before them, the balloonist Aida de Acosta, a Cuban.

He did not refrain from telling her about the difficulties these women had experienced, nor did he spare her the details of, in a few unfortunate cases, their deaths in the air. Yet he chose to emphasize their fortitude and determination despite the forces that sought to hinder women in the profession.

Upon receiving this "aviation litany," Lenora thought George's account of the gorgeous, green-eyed Harriet Quimby, American journalist and aviatrix, was the most provocative and tragic. She was riveted as she read about Quimby's achievements, and couldn't help but feel a lingering sorrow upon learning of her fate.

She imagined Harriet in her snazzy, much publicized plum-tinted jumpsuit, flying triumphantly over the English Channel, from Dover to the coast of Hardelot. The French fisherfolk running to greet her and lifting her up in victory after she had safely landed on the beach below Calais. And, then, less than three months after this remarkable feat, her tragic end.

"Winging out beyond Boston Harbor," George Hanson had written, "over Dorchester Bay, for the very last time, she steered her Blériot masterfully. She went beyond the Boston Light. And, then, she circled back to land. But she never made it back."

She was mesmerized by George's description of Bessica Raiche's hand-made silken airplane. "Picture a plane of bamboo, tied with piano wire, draped in Chinese silk. In that creation, kitelike, yet cartilage steady, she made her first solo flight. She flew without ever having a lesson."

She imagined this unusual plane as an object of art. A delicate sculpture of silk on a frame, making a music of wind.

When she came to the end of the letter, there was an enticing invitation.

If you can find your way to coming to Long Island, if you can find the courage to make the leap, I will solo you myself. I have my own little school now, and I can arrange for you to stay at my aunt Janet's house. She would be more than happy to have some company. Besides, it won't take longer, the training, that is, than two weeks. Twelve lessons total. Well, think it over. Let me know.

And then, *"Your friend, always, George H."*

PART THREE

SIX

AUTUMN 1924

A LEOPARD

*P*epe was about to saddle up his horse to begin his morning rounds. He had just rung the large bell at the house, signaling to the field hands that their workday had begun. But as he made his way along the road, he stopped. Coming toward him was an odd-looking man with braided hair, streaked white. He was dressed in beige safari jacket, baggy pants, and high-topped canvas boots. Sizing up the rangy character whose eyes seemed to be of mismatched color, Pepe silently waited until the *forastero* introduced himself. Then he asked the visitor what matter of business had brought him to La Sardinera.

"Well," replied Art Ríos, "I have a rather interesting offer for Señor Demarest. Is it possible to talk to him?"

"If you wait here for a moment," answered Pepe, with perhaps more formality than was necessary, "I will ask Don Demarest to come and meet you."

Within minutes, not having found his employer in the house, Pepe returned with Lenora, who, walking ahead of him, kept turning around to ask, "What did you say this is about and who did you say this gentleman is, and how does he know about us?" until she came face-to-face with the safari-clad stranger herself.

"I am Lenora Demarest," she offered a bit warily as she extended her hand. "I'm afraid my father is not present at the moment. May I be of help?"

"Miss Demarest, very pleased to meet you. And, yes, you might be interested in something I want to show you. An acquaintance of mine in San Juan, I believe a friend of yours, a Mr. Jonathan Mansfield, gave me some names of people on the island who might have reason to purchase my product."

Lenora, looking first at Pepe to see his reaction, then turned to the visitor somewhat suspiciously; nevertheless, she grabbed the foreman's arm and proceeded to follow the mysterious American with the twangy accent. When they reached his cart, they found that it contained a large metal cage, within which was lying a leopard. In the sun, the animal's black rosetted spots looked like inkwells, wet and sticky.

"Of course, she is tame," explained the visitor. "Until just a year ago, I worked in a *carpa*, a little traveling circus out of San Antonio, Texas." The *carpa* closed down and I traveled east to New York, where I worked for a small carnival outta Poughkeepsie. But I've left the circus business, and I've come to Puerto Rico to 'stablish other interests. She's a fine cat, and I believe a magnificent pet for someone of a particular temperament."

Lenora, squinting at the sleek, majestic animal before her, responded, "And what might that temperament be, Mr. Ríos?"

Pausing to put a blade of grass in his thin-lipped mouth, the Texan answered, "Why, Miss Demarest, an independent temperament." And he smiled, showing off pointy, tobacco-stained teeth.

"Does she have a name?"

"Oh yes. Would you believe Bendition?"

Lenora looked at the leopard, which seemed to be, in turn, studying her with equal curiousity. She walked around the cage several times and then, to Pepe's consternation, asked that the leopard be released.

Bendition, who was on a long, leather leash, docilely walked out of the cage and proceeded to lie down beneath a towering palm, stretching out languidly under the shade.

"You can pet her. Go ahead."

An hour later, after answering every manner of question regarding the caretaking of such a cat, and coming to an agreement on the price of the animal, Art Ríos left the Demarest estate without his "product."

That evening, when Henry Demarest returned home from a day trip to San Juan, he found the leopard outside, sitting regally on a rattan chair. "What on God's holy earth?" rang loud and clear, all the way to Lenora's second-floor bedroom. And within a matter of seconds, she came running out to the patio to explain.

After describing the unusual event of the morning, how Jonathan Mansfield had given a certain Texan named Art Ríos their name and address and how Lenora had felt that there was something special about the animal, how docile it seemed—after all it was an old leopard—Henry could only conclude that his daughter was afflicted these days with something far more serious than boredom. What was next? First the obsession with flying, her aloofness toward Ignacio. The never-ending acquisition of pets. Dogs and deer (how she had ever decided to bring a doe from Chautauqua to this island he would never understand). And now, this acquisition of a jungle creature.

"Lenora, my dear, do you think you can adequately handle such an animal? You are sure that it is tame?"

A DIAMOND MORE YELLOW THAN BLUE OR WHITE

Milady opened up the small, red box and looked at the square-cut jewel, a diamond more yellow in shade than blue or white, for what must have been the twentieth time. She felt slightly jittery, not only because it was the most exquisite piece of jewelry she had ever seen but because it made her think of all the contrasts in her life, the absurdities of her predicament. A gift of engagement from "Enrique," as she called her Henry.

Henry Demarest had given her the wrapped box that very afternoon with just a few words of warning, "I truly hope, my darling, that you will not disappoint me in my greatest wish." And then he had kissed her softly on the cheek and walked away.

As she sat in her sitting room, the sunlight filtering through the stained-glass windows, she thought about the moments, the hundreds of small instances, that had led to this private declaration.

She remembered the first time she had met Henry Demarest. He had been walking toward the house, wearing white pants, white shirt rolled up to the elbows, and a blue bow tie, wiping his brow with a large square handkerchief, and smiling broadly as he approached his daughter on the patio, greeting her with "Hello, my dear." It was only after he had given Lenora a quick hug that he looked at Milady and smiled, introducing himself informally and extending his hand with an apology. "I am afraid my hands are quite dirty. I have just come from the fields."

Would she have ever guessed this older man might some day send her secret, amorous epistles, wish to dance with her under the stars, take her into his arms as they lay in a hammock late at night?

She envisioned other moments when their paths had crossed in telling ways: Henry offering her a bouquet of flowers, "to make your room more sympathetic, Milady"; Henry asking her to join him and his daughter for breakfast. That morning she had blushed in shame when noticing Lenora's reaction. And then that fateful night, when Henry had visited her, during Lenora's first trip back to Driftwood. The moment when their courtship had begun. She remembered being startled by the rapping on the door of her sitting room, then opening the door and seeing Henry, book in hand, asking if he might not take a look at her pictures.

"Lovely drawings, Milady," he had commented. "And this one. Where is this?"

And Milady's tentative response. "Near my home in Mayagüez, Señor Demarest. It is sugarcane in bloom. In January, when the stalk is very high, entire fields become a silvery pink, like row after row of tinsel."

And then, "May I keep this drawing, for I would like to hang it in my study."

Their first kiss followed. So light. And brief. So unbelievable to her that, at first, she wasn't sure it was a kiss. The moment seemed a bit unreal, for in the darkness of her room, the starlight coming through an open window, Henry Demarest's dark figure had seemed to blend with other shadows. He had leaned forward, she thought, to take the little picture, but instead she had felt the push of his lips against her neck, his tobacco scent, the oriental smell of his cologne, the warmth of his breath.

This romance in shadows. It had caught her by surprise and she had tried her best to stop it. Had she ever encouraged him? She had searched her conscience, night after night, once Henry had revealed his intentions and what she discovered about herself had been upsetting. She did not feel worthy of a union with this American. She could imagine marrying a laborer, a man whose station matched her own, but she found it almost painful to be loved by someone like Henry Demarest. She felt inadequate, unsure of herself in his presence, and yet, she had somehow allowed herself to be swept up by his ardor. Was it on account of her family? Or was the real truth that this marriage would liberate her from the toils of an impoverished existence. Was it a bad thing to marry for security? Henry was a good man, and although she hadn't found the passionate romance of which she had dreamt, weren't there terribly unhappy couples everywhere, men and women who had confessed their love for one another at the start, only to find that lust could not heal the wounds of every day, the never-ending lack of money, the illnesses, loss of a job, of no

86

work, of month after month just trying to exist? Juanita, her favorite cousin. What a tragic life that poor soul had endured, all because of an intense sexual attraction. Eight years of bruises, broken ribs, and a dispirited heart. She had fallen in love, wildly and wholly, with a man whose equilibrium of spirit had never been quite right. Poor Juanita. Of what use was a marriage like hers? Henry Demarest, at the very least, was a fine man. A loving father. *Ave María*, but what would they tell Lenora? How could she, a servant—hired by the woman of the household—become the woman of the household? She felt as though she had, somehow, betrayed Enrique's daughter. Had Henry thought this through?

Opening the little box again, Milady took the ring and slipped it on her finger. The yellow diamond, against her tawny skin, was flattering and a perfect complement to her complexion. But, just as quickly, she took it off and put the ring back in its velvet box.

Opening the window of her parlor as wide as it would go, she busied herself with tidying up, patting pillows, dusting her few possessions, and watering her orchids.

A CONVERSATION

That evening, when Demarest came to Milady's room as was his habit, they talked for hours as they cuddled on the small divan. Henry gently brushed Milady's hair with his fingers, as she tried to find the words to tell him what was bothering her.

"Enrique," she began cautiously, nestling her head against his shoulder and bringing his right hand up to her lips, "I am completely overwhelmed, my love, this ring is beautiful, beyond anything that I could possibly have imagined for myself—but, truly, I must tell you I am worried about how this might affect Lenora. I would be lying if I were to tell you I do not feel somewhat *culpable*, guilty. I wonder if you understand how difficult this could be for all of us: Lenora took me in, gave me a chance to start a new life. She entrusted me with the most sacred part of her home, her relationship to you."

"But, my heart, why should our happiness mean, for my daughter, unhappiness? I do not see how my marrying you could be a problem for Lenora. I would even say that she will be delighted to have you among us . . . as family. Do not underestimate her open mind. She has quite a liberated view of the world. I am sure you have noticed."

And, then, he whispered, "Milady, you have given me such joy."

A WEDDING DATE

*J*ust after dinner, one late October evening, once Milady had served both Henry and Lenora coffee and a creamy mango flan, Henry asked Milady to sit down. The dining room was completely quiet, save for the pleasant measured ticking of a much-treasured Seth Thomas, which rested on a long oak sideboard. Lenora felt she knew what her father was about to relate; for some odd reason she had intuited the significance of this evening like no other moment in her life. Her perception at its finest; for Milady, dressed in a simple skirt, blouse, and linen apron, sat down next to Lenora and held out her hand.

Oddly enough it was only then that Lenora noticed the ring. A large, canary yellow diamond. Rare and beautiful, it caught the candlelight.

"My dear," began Henry Demarest, with the softest tone his voice could yield, "I didn't know quite how to tell you this good news, except to be plain-spoken. Milady and I are, well, we are to be married. We simply wish to share our happiness with you this evening. We feel so blessed. So immensely grateful to have found this love. But we need to have your blessing. We need, my dear, to have your blessing."

And then it was Milady's turn to speak.

"Lenora, I think I find this so much more difficult than your father, for I think this is not just *matrimonio* we are talking about this evening; but our friendship, the trust between us, creating one family of three hearts. Please, *por favor*, listen carefully to what I feel I must say to you. I never, ever, *ni por un minuto*, Lenora, believed that such a thing could be possible. I never in my life could have imagined that I would marry someone like your father. The possibility of meeting an American family like your own is something that I can only describe as *destino*. My incredible destiny. And I have prayed to *la Virgen María* for guidance. As your father has just said, we need your blessing, Lenora. I, perhaps, more than your father."

Lenora listened to Milady just as she had listened to her father, but she found herself not concentrating on their words as much as listening to the timbre of their distinct and differing voices. She felt certain that she was listening in a way that she had never listened to anything before, not to the most beautiful sonata, or the lulling, pulling reach of the midnight ocean, not to the sound of a winter's maple, creaking from the weight of ice, or the full-torso swell of a Christmas choir, or the reed-like elation of a child's surprise.

Fortunately, she found within herself a response equal to the occasion; an expression that conveyed a quiet reverence. And so, looking at her father, who was sitting across from her, and then Milady, at her side, she reached out to hold their hands. She was fighting tears and smiling. She wished desperately not to be there. And, then, she spoke. "Father, Milady, you do have my blessing."

Letting go of her father's hand, she took Milady's in both of hers, and carefully examined the diamond, remarking, "It is lovely. Special. Very rare, I think."

Then, Henry Demarest spoke again.

"Lenora, dear, Milady would so very much like for you to be her sponsor, and I am hoping that Ignacio will agree to be mine."

Lenora quietly answered, "Of course, Papa. But you have not mentioned the date? When is the ceremony?"

"We were hoping Christmas," replied Milady.

"I think a toast is fitting, no, my love?" added Henry as he kissed Milady's shaking hand.

From a corner cabinet, he took a bottle of dry sherry and poured three small glasses.

Recognizing the importance of this moment, and not letting a minute go by, Lenora quickly raised her glass, saying, "To Papa, dearest Papa, and to Milady, may you be happy, always."

That night, after she had helped Milady tidy up in the kitchen, and Henry had retired to his study, Lenora went directly to her room. She wished to be alone, not in the parlor, but in her own, large bedroom.

After she put on her favorite dressing robe, a pale blue satin, she paced the cool tiled floors as she furiously brushed her hair. Finally, getting into bed, she wept. She wept for hours. And then, realizing that she could not sleep, she read.

As if to find a way to assuage her grief, she dove into her favorite book, always a distraction, and read about the history of diamonds. Milady's ring was certainly exceptional; her father had chosen well. She wondered if Señor Iglesias had helped him. It was much larger than the ring her mother had worn. Had her father thought about the contrast?

Looking at the index of the Imbert book, she found the section on the history of diamonds and flipped to the first page of the chapter.

Several gems of world importance were mentioned: the Dresden Green Diamond (apple, moss and spring green all at once), the Briolette of India (first owned by the exquisite, shameless Eleanor of Aquitaine), the Great Blue Diamond (cursed perhaps); the Wittelsbach (gift of Philip IV of Spain to his daughter Margaret Theresa on the occasion of her wedding in 1666); the Spoonmaker (discovered in a pile of refuse, according to legend, by a Turkish fisherman who sold it to a spoonmaker for three spoons).

What was Milady doing? Was she in her room, alone, or was she with her father? Were they at that very moment embracing somewhere in the darkness? Lenora's cheeks were burning; and she felt a prickly rash develop on her chest and neck.

Although she attempted to accept the idea of her father's love for a woman other than her mother, she found her heart resisting. This new affection was such an affront to her mother's memory. She could think of nothing but her mother's grace and beauty, her extraordinary spirit.

She stumbled on a paragraph about the great Koh-i-Noor. "A diamond of such notoriety it is, without question," opined Imbert, "the most famous diamond of the ages. Originally 600 carats, legend has it that this rare, fabled stone was discovered on a baby's forehead; not just any boy infant, mind you, but the brow of Karna, offspring of the Vedic sun god. The child was taken to court, whereupon the stone was taken from his wisened brow and placed upon the sacred statue of Shiva. Over the third eye. Symbolic of englightenment."

Would Milady wisely handle her new status? Not only that of wife but also mistress of a large estate? How would she comport herself? Remarkable and strange, really; the whole thing. Would they treat each other as sisters or friends? Certainly not as stepmother and daughter. It seemed impossible.

She continued perusing the book before her. "Not until the year 1304 is the Koh-i-Noor mentioned in any text. We are told that it was in the possession of a rajah from Malwa. After several centuries of ownership by the Mughals, the diamond would change hands again; as war booty. Of all the forthcoming twists and turns, vagaries of fate, and ironies of human wealth this is what would happen when the shah of Persia, Nader Shad, sacked Delhi in 1739: Having vanquished his enemy, the shah held a ceremonial dinner for Muhammad Shah, in which, according to the custom of the time each ruler proffered his turban to the other. A peace-offering of sorts. Lo and behold, beneath the multi-pleated turban of the vanquished ruler lay the great Koh-i-Noor. And thus the magical diamond, also known as 'The Mountain of Light,' once again changed hands."

Having read in a state of nervous exhaustion and bewilderment, Lenora stopped her reading, closed her book, and finally, after much tossing and turning, drifted into sleep.

A CONFESSION

*I*t would have happened sooner or later, their heart to heart, but never the way Lenora imagined it. And, yet, had she paid closer attention to Milady the night of her father's announcement, she might have better understood Milady's feelings. For in hindsight, Lenora realized that Milady seemed almost as upset and worried as she herself had been that evening. She recalled that she had taken Milady's hand in hers, not so much because she wished to examine her engagement ring, but because she saw the trembling fingers, the sweaty brow, and somehow, without being fully aware of her intentions, had sought to comfort her.

Yes, it had happened quite unexpectedly, their long and forthright conversation. Had Lenora not been in the kitchen in the early hours of the morning, getting herself a cup of *manzanilla* tea, she never would have heard Milady crying. It hadn't been exactly heart-wrenching the weeping, but rather curious, as the sounds were muffled, held back by restraint. Lenora had moved closer to Milady's door to listen, not without a tinge of shame.

Then, suddenly, without any warning at all, the door had swung open, and the two women, startled, had let out little screams.

Lenora remembered that her ears were on fire, so embarrassed was she by her indiscretion. Milady looked miserable, her hair was wet and stringy on her face. Eyes bloodshot and red. It had been Milady who apologized first with, "Oh, Lenora, forgive me. Are you all right?" And, "Did I hurt you? Are you sure?" Then, it was Lenora who offered, she had to admit, a feeble, and not entirely valid, explanation. "I was worried about you and was just about to knock. *¿Milady, qué te pasa?*"

Milady was shaking her head. So, Lenora asked her to sit down and offered her the camomile infusion she had just prepared.

In those quiet hours, the distraught woman bore her soul; all the while sipping tea and nibbling chocolate biscuits. How frightened she was by the prospect of being Enrique's wife; she simply did not have "*la educación.*" Yes, yes, she could clean and cook, but what about her duties as hostess? *¿Entiendes? Señ-or-a de-la-ca-sa.* Henry loved to entertain, and all those important people, poets, politicians, *gente sabia, sabia,* what could she possibly say to such *gente refinada?* Didn't her father understand that she was simple, *sencilla?* "You know what that means, Señorita Lenora. I am so worried."

Lenora, struck by the honesty of Milady's words, her insecurity about the life to which she was headed in a mere matter of weeks, was much moved by her vulnerability, and soon she found herself reassuring the housekeeper again and again that it would not be so difficult and that she would help her, and not to worry. So, in the course of their long chat, Lenora found that her resentments were slowly disappearing, too.

Eventually, what had begun as a confessional, at least for Milady, evolved into easy banter about the wedding itself. The Puerto Rican housekeeper-soon-to-be-stepmother asked Lenora to help her find a gown. The women talked animatedly about what food should be served and whom to invite and whether the ceremony should take place in the morning or the evening, and should there be a flower girl, a band.

And Lenora thought that for "something borrowed" and good luck, she would lend Milady a treasured bracelet of brilliant Chinese jade and pearls.

A QUESTION AT THE WEDDING

Henry Demarest, dapper in an English suit of fine beige wool, starched white cotton shirt and white bow tie, and his Puerto Rican bride, Milady García-Enríquez, resplendent in her white silk gown and lace mantilla veil, were married in a civil ceremony on a sunny, mild Christmas morning, with Lenora and Ignacio at their sides. For the occasion, Palés-Matos, who, by then, had become a good friend of the family, read aloud *"Soneto Pascual"* in honor of the sacramental day. But however heartfelt and solemn the special moment, there was a bit of unexpected drama. Just as the young poet began the third stanza of Rubén Darío's verse with *"Esa visión en mí se alza y se multiplica,"* a shriek of terror halted the polished performance. Pepe's smallest child, Rosita, who had become a very excitable eight-year-old, started crying, all the while jumping up and down and pointing hysterically as Bendition made an appearance among the bridal party.

The child, while not knowing what type of hefty creature was before her, did know enough to understand it was not a cuddly thing like Lenora's fluffy English sheepdog, Jason.

By now, of course, word about Lenora's eccentricity—*"¡esa mujer, de verdad, tiene una pantera en casa, fíjate tú, está loca!"* had circulated among the residents of Dorado, and everyone who knew the family was well aware that Señorita Demarest loved the creature just as much as she loved her gold-toothed dog, her *venado*, her parrots. But no one had expected to see Bendition walk among them that day of Christmas cheer, and there was a general sense of relief when the creature, led quickly away by its mistress, was out of sight for good.

After Palés Matos resumed and finished his recitation, the bridal party and their twenty-five guests happily strolled, to the accompaniment of three guitarists playing traditional *villancicos*, toward a long white tent—erected next to the beach—for the Christmas luncheon.

Milady's parents, Los Señores García, were awestruck upon entering the canopied sanctuary. It seemed that they were standing inside a botanical garden, so lush and rich with greenery was the interior. Lenora, with Pepe's help, had decorated the makeshift space, using small trees, lemon and lime, to add a festive touch. Thick garlands of white carnations braided with dark green ribbon streamers, crisscrossed from one corner of the tent to the other. Delicate china, crystal, and large silver bowls of oranges and fragrant orange blossoms rested upon the long table.

When all the guests had finally entered the heavenly scented space and had found their seats, Lenora asked the waiters—on loan from a restaurant in San Juan—to begin serving the meal. Milady had decided on the menu herself: grilled lobster tail, with garlic-butter dipping sauce, chicken in sherry (one of Henry's favorite dishes), breadfruit croquettes, fancy rice with raisins and almonds, and anise-flavored *chayote* squash. All of this was washed down with the best of Spanish sparkling wines.

Henry Demarest could not stop staring at his bride. Her beauty, set off by the luminous silk of her formal Spanish wedding dress, overwhelmed him. He studied the shine of her auburn hair, her caramel-colored eyes, her delicate dark lips, the unusual shade of which he had pondered, secretly, day and night. Were they the color of plum? Such a sweet and vulnerable face. Heart-shaped. Such a mild disposition. Taking his wife's left hand, he brought it to his lips and whispered to his bride, who blushed and put her head down.

Everybody oohed and aahed when the wedding cake, covered in pale pink icing and a profusion of scarlet roses, was wheeled in on a little cart. Although Milady had wanted to make it herself, Lenora had adamantly objected. The five-tiered delight, before their eyes, of heavy cream, almond paste, eggs, and sugar, had been the handiwork of an elderly deaf woman in town, a baker known as Carmen la Buena.

The magnificent cake had taken three days to complete. Carmen had labored over its design (a bell), scent (jasmine-rose), and flavor (marzipan-vanilla). A highly regarded baker who had worked her trade for forty years, she had scoured every cookery book in her possession, finally discovering a nineteenth-century Italian recipe. It was an annotation to this recipe, by its author, that had convinced Carmen she should search no more. "This cake," opined a certain Giovanna Belli, "will make you cry, it is so good. Celestial. Rich, creamy, yet not too sweet. It is my opinion that this sweet derives from Arabic-Sicilian origin."

It was during the eating of cake and making of toasts—"May your love protect you, keep you safe," "To Henry, to his singular intellect and to Milady, to her dazzling beauty," "To the loveliest couple Dorado has ever known,"—that Ignacio finally made up his mind to ask Lenora a question he had rehearsed in his mind at least one hundred times in various combinations of words and in varying august tones throughout that long year.

Just a few days before, a conversation with his father had, perhaps, emboldened him to do so.

"And what of *la Señorita Demarest?*" the elder had asked. "Given what seems to be your complete devotion to *esta americana*—although I would rather see you married to a woman of our own background, at least, at the very least, someone Catholic—I had thought you might be *prometidos*, engaged, by now. Well, what is it?"

"Ay, *papá*, truthfully, I do not know how to answer such a question."

Ignacio, rubbing his large, tanned hands, had looked down at the polished terra-cotta floor. What could he say? He was, he felt, unprepared to explain the quandary in which he found himself, as he really did not know the truth of things. It wasn't that he thought Lenora indifferent to his attentions; quite the contrary, in fact. Why, anybody with eyes could see that she fussed over him when he was at La Sardinera. She enjoyed riding with him on Sundays. Did they not engage in easy conversation? She listened with the utmost feminine attention to his every word. And she dressed with flair. Her elegant clothing accentuated her womanly figure in the most seductive way. Teasingly. And she wore the *enseigne* fairly often in his presence. She must have, as he guessed she would, come to know about the gem through her reading or, perhaps, that jeweler—*what was his name?*—in San Juan. She understood the function of the piece; it was obvious, as she occasionally pinned it to her sun hat. But she never once, not once, mentioned anything about it to him. How could that be?

"I suppose I could answer by saying that I am waiting a few more months. I believe the appropriate time has simply not come. And I have yet to speak to Señor Demarest about it."

"*Pues, bien, hijo.* But if I were you I would not wait too long."

Nodding slowly, the young man had stood up and rushed out of his father's office.

Taking advantage of a sudden lull in the festivities, Ignacio excused himself and left the tent. Standing at the edge of the beach, he took a few puffs on his cigar, and thought the matter over once again. Was this the moment for which he had waited? If he were to lose the spirit of this day, the momentum set in motion by the cele-bratory mood, he might never again be given such an opportunity to ask for Lenora's hand. How to do it, though. Should he propose dur-ing dancing or should he lead her away, to someplace private, quiet?

It was then that Lenora, taking Rosita by the hand, walked out of the tent and waved at Ignacio.

"I'm taking Rosita to the house for a while; do you want to join us?" And Ignacio, smiling, quickly went to them, saying, "*Claro, claro.* Of course."

As they walked the short distance to the house's interior court-yard, Lenora felt Ignacio staring at her. She wondered if he disap-proved of her appearance, particularly the *bandeau* that she had worn for the occasion.

"Ignacio, do you not like my tiara?"

"Why would you think such a thing? No, no. On the contrary, I think it is beautiful. Not quite as beautiful as its wearer, but lovely. And touching the band on her forehead, he asked, "What kind of stone?"

"They are peridots."

"Well, they suit you. They really do."

While Rosita, dressed in a multilayered frock of white organza—a gift from Lenora for the occasion—played in the court-yard, chasing after the dog, and singing songs, Lenora and Ignacio sat in the shade and watched. Ignacio, trying to be discreet, took in Lenora's presence, every bit of it; from her diaphanous beige gown of silk and satin, to the green velvet trimming of her hem, her matching slippers. She was stunning. It was the moment.

Taking Lenora's hand in his own, he began, "I love you, I love you ... with all of my being. I ache for you. ..."

AFTER THE WEDDING

*B*ecause she could not sleep, she got up from her bed, put on her robe, and quickly went outside.

She walked around the back of the house and stood just feet away from where the tent had been positioned hours earlier. All tokens of the Christmas wedding had been taken down and removed, except for the potted citrus trees, which remained in the sand, close to shore. She looked east, along the bay. In the distance was the *shake-shake-shake* of maracas and the strains of a *cuatro* guitar, and singing; the singing of laborers who had drunk too much *pitorro*, the men who were working their land; those mild-mannered people who had come, family by family, to ask to be part of *la finca*.

As if called by the music, laughter, and *timbal*, she started walking up the beach, slowly, in the hours after midnight. She wondered whose tenor strains she heard far off in the distance. Was it Budda? Manuel? Antonio? Probably Antonio. He had a natural singing voice that, during the weekdays, coaxed others into humming, too, among the endless rows of grapefruit, and *caña*, and *chinas*. She loved to listen to their songs about the mountains and the country, loves and disappointments.

Seventy men now worked for them. Their children she had come to adore, particularly Pepe's brood. Rosita, especially, of course. And even the oldest boy, Beto, who was a tad sneaky.

Walking slowly toward the little town at the far end of the bay, she came upon a large piece of driftwood, its two ends sharp and daggerlike. Carefully, so as not to tear her robe, she sat down on the smooth curve of the sea-worn trunk, and looked out to the darkness of the ocean.

She did not love Ignacio, of this she was certain. She might have told him the truth, that she had much to do before she contemplated matrimony. And especially with a man whose views of women were *so traditional.* She knew what he would want from her: children, a lot of children. A life of order with everything in its place, with her in her place. Could he not see that she was different? So easy, it might have been to finally say, "I'm sorry, Ignacio, but I do not wish to marry, or at least not yet." Why had she allowed herself to be so weak? Instead, flustered and completely taken aback by his offer of marriage, she had feebly answered, "Ignacio, I'm, well, overwhelmed. And flattered, of course. I don't know what to say. Let's think about this further, shall we?" He had seemed so wounded by her slow and hesitant response.

PART FOUR

SEVEN

SPRING 1925

THE SILVER SARDINE

 nergized by love and the support of his young wife, Henry Demarest concerned himself the first year of his second marriage with several new constructions at the plantation. Milady had persuaded him to build a primary school for the children of La Sardinera's employees, and she had also convinced him to build a small clinic for the townspeople, which they would call La Casa Verde or The Green House.

After a decade of strenuous labor, the plantation was, finally, profitable. Lenora, he believed, was making great improvements in the management and productivity of the enterprise. As grapefruit harvesting occurred throughout the year, she had devised a monthly system for the transportation of the fruit: first it was packed in crates, next it was taken by carriage to the railway station and loaded there for delivery to San Juan. Once in the capital, Jonathan Mansfield, whose company oversaw the transfer of fruit to the ships in the port, completed the operation.

Because there was now more demand for La Sardinera citrus,

Demarest had built a larger packing plant, consisting of several rooms, across the road from the estate, adjacent to the fields.

In the packing plant, redolent with the sharp scent of just picked *toronja*, yellow green in its barely ripened state, women of various ages, sun-wrinkled grandmothers as well as smooth-skinned young girls of eighteen, sat and told love stories while they meticulously wrapped grapefruits in white silken paper.

One day it had occurred to Lenora that the silken wraps should have a decoration, something to advertise the origin of the fruit itself. Perhaps a shield with the name of Dorado or La Sardinera.

She decided to pay a visit to their business associate in San Juan for advice. Mansfield had been helpful to the Demarests at every stage of La Sardinera's development, and Lenora had learned that she could count on his opinion with confidence when it came to marketing matters. Even so, she had been unprepared for Mansfield's exceptionally keen interest in the ornamental aspect of the citrus wraps themselves.

"I'm afraid that won't do," he had replied upon seeing the simple drawing that Lenora presented. "You'll need something distinctive. A symbol, perhaps, that directly connects your grapefruit to the plantation. A design element that distinguishes your grapefruit from all others. Here, take a look at this. You might get a few ideas."

Having been handed a voluminous album so stuffed with wrappings of every shade and size and material, she was convinced that she had better take her time and study the contents. And, so, she settled into one of Mansfield's leather chairs and started looking at each wrapper.

Most of the decorative tissues were from orange and lemon orchards in various Spanish towns, especially Valencia and Murcia. The complexity and artistry of the wrappings were impressive in detail and diversity. There were mythological, historical, and zoological designs and those that celebrated heraldic motifs, with ornate shields in gold and royal blue. A few showed beautiful women wearing mantillas and horsemen dressed in three-cornered hats. Other designs appealed to children, featuring sprites and canaries. There were designs of religious iconography—the Virgin Mary, Capuchin monks, and saints. Flower designs, oriental designs, and designs with seductresses, scantily clad.

When, after several hours, Lenora left the Mansfield offices, the image of a tiger standing on flowers and another of a translucent princess-sylph were very much on her mind.

As she thought about La Sardinera, its peculiarities and singularities, she pondered a few designs that might be marketable. She considered a leopard, a dog, a little deer, a green parrot. She contemplated using the image of the estate itself, a palm tree, a shell. Perhaps it might be prudent to use a drawing of her father. Or maybe an airplane.

And then, suddenly, it occurred to her that she might utilize the image of a small sardine, silver in color, just like the sardines of La Sardinera Bay.

It was, thus, that Milady and Lenora sat down one night in the

dining room of the house with Milady's paints and pencils and discussed various combinations of wording and imagery.

In the end, they both agreed on a design that seemed just right.
Bold and clear, yet lovely enough to pass for a picture that might be
framed: A meticulously rendered small sardine in silver coloration
against a cream background, around which was the lettering *Citrus par-
adisi* in gold, La Sardinera in pink, and Product of Puerto Rico in
crimson red.

EIGHT

AUTUMN 1925

ROSITA

Gradually, as Milady began to assume more wifely duties at La Sardinera during the autumnal months of 1925, Lenora found that she preferred to spend the better part of her day at the packing plant or riding in the fields. Her father wasn't quite the active man that he had been when they had first come to Dorado's shores. His back had been bothering him of late. It seemed, too, that in a matter of months he had slowed down considerably, and so Milady had encouraged him to spend more of his time at the hospital. Henry's medical expertise was greatly appreciated by townspeople and La Sardinera employees, as there were no other doctors upon whom to rely in that remote and densely populated countryside.

Henry spent his working hours tending to broken wrists and sprained ankles, delivering babies, stitching up gashes, and ministering to any number of patients whose illnesses ran from flu to more serious, life-threatening afflictions.

It fell to Lenora, with Pepe's assistance, to make sure that the vast lands of the *finca* were well maintained.

The day began early. Usually, she and the foreman would take a horsedrawn carriage out to the small village of Dorado to collect whatever supplies they might need, as well as to retrieve their mail, and then having returned to the estate, they would saddle up their horses and survey the plantation.

The grapefruit pickers rarely complained, but Lenora liked to chat with them anyway to find out what concerns they had about their duties, their salaries, and also to learn from them. She was intrigued by their country wisdom. "Señorita Demarest," one of them might say, "do you know this proverb? 'Tell everybody your business and the devil will do it for you.' And another might add, "'Those who are right need not talk loudly.'" And yet someone else, "'Life without a friend is death without a witness.'" She could spend hours listening to the men ply one another with words of advice regarding, perhaps, someone's sick father, or a mother-in-law who meddled way too much, or an American government that didn't seem to understand their customs, that didn't seem to care enough about the Puerto Rican people.

It was in this way, by observation and listening, that Lenora came to discern the nature of the country folk who were responsible for helping her make a success of the farm. They were a beautiful people. A bit timid. Devoutly religious. Disciplined and generous.

Sometimes, Lenora would share a lunch with them. Finding an amenable spot, they would sit on the ground and nibble on the homemade treats prepared by dedicated wives and adoring mothers. Pedro might have a bit of roasted chicken and rice, Juan some sausages. There might be a hunk of Spanish cheese, some pork. Vegetables from their gardens. Lots of freshly baked bread and *empanadillas* filled with crab and shrimp, hot peppers, and potatoes.

It was during a congenial picnic lunch of this sort that tragedy struck their little community.

When Lenora heard the ringing of the bell, a bell that was rung without exception three times daily—in the morning to announce the start of work, at lunchtime, and at the end of the day—she and Pepe knew that something at the house was wrong.

Having jumped onto their horses, Lenora and her foreman quickly rode the mile path that led from the grapefruit fields to the estate, whereupon they saw Miss Machado, the teacher of the new little school, in hysterics and crying uncontrollably.

After Miss Machado finally regained her composure, she spoke. They learned that Rosita had wandered off during playtime and, most likely, thinking that the water looked so cool on such a very hot muggy morning, had entered a spot on the bay that was rough. By the time her classmates had realized their little friend was not among them at the end of recess, it had been too late. The young teacher had found the child lifeless on the sandy beach.

GOING TO LONG ISLAND

*E*scape was not the notion that ordinarily came to Lenora's mind. But that was what she wanted. Her father's marriage, Milady's new role in their home, Rosita's passing, Ignacio's persistent entreaties and her inability to give him a direct answer; each event had somehow worked upon her to the point where all she thought about was getting away from Puerto Rico for a while.

She had planned, as usual, to go to Driftwood in the autumn, but had changed her mind when she concluded that George Hanson was making a serious attempt to help her achieve her goal of racing the sky.

And, so, shortly after Rosita's death, she had written to her aviator pen pal and accepted his offer of twelve flying lessons.

An enthusiastic letter from George quickly followed in which he explained the particulars of the training she would receive, plane model she would use for practice, and the details of her housing arrangement with "Aunt Janet." Lenora, who had had somewhat hesitant about accepting lodging in a stranger's home, had been persuaded when she read George's one-page paragraph about his aunt's large house and winning personality.

"Lenora," he had written,

do not think that you will be a prisoner of Zenda at Janet Rowan's house. Although she is no spring chicken, my aunt is a formidable lady, a pioneer of sorts, you could say. She was the first woman in town to get her flying license (I taught her), she has her own very successful business (a floral and antique shop) and she has been known to have a few bourbons with the boys, after a long day's work. Trust me. I know the two of you will get along famously. And you'll have a comfortable room, three decent meals a day. The house is a mammoth place, with more rooms than she needs, and a fifteen-minute walk away from the airstrip. What more could you want?

What more could she want, it was true. And so, on the day she had received his upbeat missive, she had decided on her itinerary. She would spend a few days in New York City on La Sardinera business. Then she would take the train out to Hempstead. And after she had gotten her license, she would travel on to Chautauqua to spend the summer at the lake.

It was all very simple. She would, of course, have to talk to her father about it. But these days, he had shown a change of heart toward all of her "chattering about those flying machines." He had even agreed to accompany her to an air show in San Juan, and seemed thrilled about the prospect of seeing those pilots "loop the loop." It was, most likely, Milady's benignant influence on him. Although it was hard for her to admit, she had never seen her father happier.

PART FIVE

NINE

SPRING AND
SUMMER 1926

APRIL MORNING

On a clear and mild Sunday morning in April, Lenora left her small hotel near Gramercy Park, got into a cab, and went directly to the train station.

The visit to New York City had not been as successful as she had hoped. While several premier specialty grocers had decided to carry La Sardinera grapefruit, most of the hotel managers with whom she had met had told her that the Puerto Rican citrus was far too tart and small to serve in their fine eateries.

Lenora rode along Fifth Avenue, thinking about one kindly manager's suggestion. "Why not try London? I think the British have a fondness for a more bitter-tasting fruit than we do; at least that has been my observation." Perhaps he was right. She should look into it.

As soon as she arrived at Grand Central, she found a porter to carry her bags and bought her ticket to Hempstead Plains. Then, being told that the train was just about to leave, she rushed to the appropriate platform.

Within minutes, the train was on its way, and Lenora, sitting next to a window, settled into her comfortable seat and began to read.

At George's urging, she had brought along several books on New York State geography, and two topographical charts. "You must become familiar with the land," he had written, if you want to be a first-class pilot." Unfolding one of the maps, she began to memorize county names and lakes, and rivers. She thought about George. Would he be as handsome as she last remembered him? Would he be at the train station alone or with his aunt?

Looking out the window, she saw the trees in mint renewal, brandishing forsythia and lilacs.

LUNCH WITH JANET

S eeing how it's Sunday, we can't fly today," said George, as they sped along a country highway toward Janet Rowan's house. "Here, the church people don't like the idea of flying on the sabbath, so, tomorrow we'll begin. We'll start first thing in the morning, if that's all right with you." He was smiling at Lenora, in that way of his, a sweet grin that seemed at odds with his angular face. "I just know that you and Janet are going to get along real fine. You'll see."

She noticed that the aviator was a careful driver. And considerate. As they crossed a little bridge, past a field of neglected narcissi, or drove through forest, he would slow down to comment on a site that caught his fancy or recount an anecdote, sometimes relating what misfortune might have befallen whom and when. "This bridge in the winter gets pretty slick and last year ol' Ben Carrey drove his car straight off and ended up in the stream below; luckily the old fellow only broke an arm." "See that oak tree up ahead, that's where I used to practice archery when I was a kid," or "In spring my aunt picks fiddleheads and in June the sweetest wild strawberries in that field."

And then, before she knew it, they were driving down a shade-dappled lane with several large houses, finally stopping at an elaborately fashioned gate, painted white. "We're here," he said, as he grabbed her luggage and helped Lenora out of the car.

On the left post, an ornately lettered sign read: ROWAN'S FLOWERS AND ANTIQUES.

"Come on," urged George, as he took Lenora's hand, "we're running a little late, and Aunt Janet is a punctual woman, especially when it comes to Sunday lunch."

They quickly walked the gravel drive. The house, boxy and imposing, was not set too far from the road, but it was well hidden by a very high hedge of juniper. On the brick-laid stoop, two large granite urns were stuffed with fern, blooming myrtle, and a shock of daffodils.

George hit the doorbell, stomped his feet quickly, and cleared his throat. Within seconds, an elderly woman with well-coiffed silver hair, dressed in a navy gabardine suit, came to the door.

"Welcome, welcome, children," greeted Janet, as she hugged, first, George and, then, Lenora. "Do come in."

Upon entering the sunlit slate-floored entry, Janet took Lenora's coat and asked George if he minded taking her luggage to the guest bedroom.

"Lenora, if you are up to it," she added, "I'd like to show you around the house before we have luncheon."

And, so, while George disappeared with Lenora's bags, Janet, taking Lenora's hand, led her around the first floor of her home.

Finely painted porcelain jardinieres were filled to overflowing with white lilies, the scent of Easter everywhere. It seemed, in fact, that the entire house was aglow and shimmery. Copper-veined glass mirrors lined the living room walls. Sunlight flashed around. Graceful, overstuffed armchairs, sofas, and divans faded into one another's shades of apricot and red. Upon the gleaming wooden floors were scattered oriental rugs in a cream hue that Janet described as "Isabeline."

"My pride and joy, dear, is, of course, my shop."

Down a small hall off the entry was a wing that looked entirely different from the rest of the house, as it seemed invested with all the colors and moods of the world. Two square rooms connected by a wide archway. To the left, the scent of roses, tangerines, sweet peas and cinnamon, cloves and eucalyptus. To the right a sea of so many objects it was nearly impossible to decipher the size of the space. There were crystal lanterns, silver vases, marble statues, urns, paintings, floor lamps, rockers and benches, chests with nacre inlay, tables with mosaic tops, and beautiful glassware. Richly designed tapestries hung on every wall.

"Most of my objects are English and Italian," explained Janet.

"There will be plenty of time in the next few weeks for you to take a better look. But now, let us have our lunch, shall we?"

After quickly freshening up, Lenora joined George and his aunt in the dining room. The lunch was simple but delicious. Roast chicken, creamed carrots with parsley, a vinegary cucumber salad. And tart lemon pie with chantilly cream for dessert.

There was much to talk about that day. Janet wished to know about the island of Puerto Rico. "Is the flora as glorious as I have read?" And she asked Lenora about the grapefruit business. "What is it like, my dear, to be in a place so far from civilization?" To which George, interrupting, responded, "I'm sorry, Aunt Janet, but the island is far from being an uncivilized place. Why, the history of the island is a rich and fascinating one; Spanish for the most part. And, therefore, unfamiliar to most Americans."

The conversation rambled from the particulars of Puerto Rico to Janet Rowan's adventures in the sky. "I'll have you know, Lenora, that I learned to fly in 1920, just six years ago. For the pure and simple fun of it. And I am darn good, too. You're in the best of hands. Even though he is my favorite nephew, the truth is George Hanson is one mighty fine pilot and teacher." And, then, as if an afterthought, she added, "I can't help but notice that you do like jewelry. Just a bit of superstitious counsel. Take along a little charm whenever you are flying; it will be your lucky amulet. A locket, a bracelet, something." And as she touched the collar of her suit, she said, "I always wear this little silver dragonfly whenever I go up."

A NATURAL

$\mathcal{L}$enora came to know the regulars at the airfield during the first week of lessons. They were mostly young men who lived near Hempstead, men for whom flying planes was much more a matter of mechanics and science than an exciting diversion. Nearly all of them had been "aces" in the war.

After a long day of flying, they would gather at the hangar and swap stories—what they called "ground flying"—while working on their planes, cleaning parts, repairing broken lines, examining their engines. A bottle of whiskey might be passed around, tales of mishap becoming slightly exaggerated. With each swig from a circulated flask, stories of crashes on roofs, dead-stick landings, imperfect stunts, running out of fuel over water, acquired mythic proportions. Feeling somewhat excluded from this club, Lenora stood close enough to them to glean precious information but not so near as to seem conspicuous.

By the time Lenora had learned how to control the plane on land and follow a straight line, she had come to know various plane models, each with its own weaknesses and strengths, that were kept at George Hanson's flying school. She had decided that the perfect machine for her was the Curtiss P-1, even though George had tried his best to push her toward the Ryan M-1, an even newer model.

Late one Saturday afternoon, Lenora got up her nerve to talk to a group of veteran flyers about the possibility of solo flights across the Atlantic and who among them was the likeliest to attempt such a feat. The men began to speculate about a fellow named Charles Lindbergh. "I have heard him talk about it all year. And from what

I've seen—I met him at an air meet in Chicago—the guy has just about as good a chance as any. He's a serious flyer. Stoic. Very methodical. No slipups with him, ever."

It was during this conversation that George strode up to the group and said to Lenora, "You handle that Curtiss like no one I have ever seen. You, quite simply, are a natural-born flyer."

That her instructor and friend would honor her with such a vote of confidence in front of his buddies, a few of whom were not so positively inclined toward "women in the sky," was not lost on her. She felt immensely proud and grateful.

That day was special for another reason. A young aviatrix named Amelia Earhart had unexpectedly landed at the school. She had been running low on fuel and, after spotting an orange-painted air-marker on a large barn rooftop for George Hanson's field, followed the two-mile southeast coordinates to Hempstead.

Lenora headed toward Amelia's plane as it was landing. The ash-blond aviatrix was sporting trousers, a plaid shirt, crumpled leather jacket, and brightly patterned blue-and-red scarf. She wore an odd-looking bracelet made of bone with silver flecks on her right wrist. Amelia's hair was a tousled mess. As she jumped out, she extended her hand and introduced herself, saying, "Amelia Earhart. Pleased to meet you."

The two women began an animated conversation that was more than courteous, returning often to the discussion of the various challenges facing women flyers. "I'm thinking of starting a club for us gals, a kind of flying association. Do you want to join?" asked Amelia, brightly.

Before night had fallen, they had exchanged addresses and phone numbers; Lenora extending, in addition, an invitation to her Chautauqua home in July. "There is a golf course a few miles from my house that serves quite well as a landing strip. And, well, I would be really happy if you came. There is plenty to do there, what with all the cultural events, fine musicians, notable thinkers, and speakers. You won't be bored, I promise you."

Given that it was so late in the afternoon, Lenora asked her new friend if she might not like to have dinner with her that evening. She was sure that Janet wouldn't mind the extra company.

By the time they arrived at Janet's house that night, the two women were sharing confidences as if they were the best of friends. And as Lenora had predicted, her elderly hostess was delighted to entertain another aviatrix. While Lenora showed Amelia to her room, Janet quickly prepared a simple spread of butter rolls, sweet pickles, tuna salad, and tomatoes from the garden.

Later, as they began to devour their meal, Janet turned to Amelia with a dimpled smile. "Tell me something of yourself, my dear."

"Well," began Amelia, "I have a job at a settlement house in Boston. It's near Chinatown. I do social work. Mainly, I help Syrian immigrants. I teach them English, try to find them employment. I truly enjoy my work, but I am trying to spend as much time as possible in my plane. There is nothing that makes me happier than flying."

"Wonderful, dear," answered the older woman. "I think you and Lenora have such interesting lives ahead of you. Women have so many possibilities for fulfillment these days. Ah, yes."

Janet looked at the beautiful women at her side, admiring their youth and ambition. "Ladies," she suddenly asked. "I wonder: do you play poker?"

FALLING PETALS

There was much laughter and gentle teasing at Janet's party in honor of Lenora. Among the guests were several of the "boys" from George Hanson's school as well as a few of Janet's favorite and most loyal customers, among them a teacher of Latin, a Miss Woodward, and the town's first woman pediatrician. George was buoyant, Lenora on top of the world. That morning "the blond from Puerto Rico" as the aviators at the school had come to call her, had gotten her pilot's license, after two weeks, twelve lessons, ten hours in the sky. And she had passed her test with the highest of recommendations.

Champagne was served in long-stemmed Venetian flutes, along with an assortment of hot and cold hors d'oeuvres, tidbits of cheese and sausage, ham pie and aspic. Majolica vases filled with wild violets decorated tables. And warmed by the effects of food and wine, as well as the good wishes and generosity of Janet and her friends, Lenora had allowed herself to feel what she had kept in check so long, in differing ways: the undeniable phsyicality of her attraction to George Hanson.

The aviator, dressed in gray wool slacks, white shirt, and a pale yellow sweater, seemed, on that evening, particularly masculine. And

Lenora, perhaps for the first time in her life, experienced a state of near swooning.

Well past midnight, after everyone had left and all the plates had been taken away, the last light and candle extinguished, something happened that convinced Lenora she was in love.

George Hanson, taking advantage of Lenora's somewhat tipsy disposition, the absence of well-wishers, and welcome silence, led her to the flower shop, which beckoned with its tranquil privacy. They sat down on a satin-covered love seat. Taking Lenora's chin in his hand, George turned her head toward the moonlight coming through a large bay window. Outside pink petals floated down from the branches of a tulip tree. In an instant, they fell into each other's arms, caressing tenderly.

FOURTH OF JULY

Walking alone through the shaded, quiet grounds at Chautauqua Institution—deemed by Theodore Roosevelt "the most American place in America"—Lenora thought about the lecture she had just attended. The title of the presentation had been advertised in *The Chautauquan Daily* as "One Hundred Ways to See the World." There couldn't have been a more apt description for what she had heard.

The speaker, an elderly yet energetic photographer from New York City, had paced excitedly around the stage, his long white hair flopping in his face. "Seeing the world through a camera lens," he said, as he exhibited photographs he had taken in Africa, "has nothing to do with reality. Inherent in the process of picture-taking is the prejudice of the heart."

Lenora, not unlike the other attendees, had been impressed by his stimulating presentation as well as by the artistry of his pictures. In fact, so appreciative was his public that he received the highest compliment offered at the Institution: the waving of white handkerchiefs, known affectionately as "the Chautauqua salute." She could not stop thinking about one of his photos: the image of a woman in Tangier, her face and body enshrouded in black cloth, walking down a crowded street as if she existed to be ignored.

As she headed toward her car, parked near the main gate of the grounds, she admired the little gardens lining the narrow brick lanes, the felicity of orange gladiolus everywhere, and the pink gingerbread-trimmed homes. In just a few hours, Amelia Earhart would be arriving from Boston to spend the Fourth of July with her.

Ever since she had met the likable social-worker-turned-aviatrix at the Hempstead airfield, Lenora had felt that there was a particularly strong bond between them. She and Amelia shared a similar philosophy toward life, an understanding of risk and personal fulfillment. "We women must try to do things as men have tried," Amelia had declared boldly the first day they had met.

It was a gorgeous, almost cool, sunny morning, the sky without clouds—the kind of day for which Chautauqua County summers were known. The act of driving down country roads and lakeside byways was a pleasure. Why so few women took up motoring as a sport, thought Lenora, was just a mystery. As she drove up to the house, she stopped abruptly, taken aback by the landscape's radiance. The garden—that had been her mother's treasure—was in full and brilliant bloom.

She had asked a neighbor who vacationed at the lake, a dentist named Thorsten Bloomberg, from nearby Jamestown, to help her swath the house in flags and cheerful bunting. Old Glory was waving from the back porch, the garage, and across the flagstone terrace at the side.

She parked the car and walked around to the front of the house to see if he had decorated there, as well. And when she turned the corner, there stood Amelia, high on a ladder, helping Dr. Bloomberg with the ruffled red, white, and blue banners.

"Amelia, well, my goodness, I wasn't expecting you until two o'clock or so. How did you manage to find this place? I was planning on picking you up at the golf course." And then she quickly added, "Oh, Dr. Bloomberg, you have done a magnificent job with the trimming. The house looks every inch a patriotic landmark."

Bloomberg nodded. "Much obliged."

And, then, Amelia spoke. "Well, I decided to leave a little earlier this morning, and when I got to the field—I landed on the fourteenth fairway—a nice golfer offered to drive me to your house. A young fellow named Steve Roberts. He said he knew your family."

"You must be starving. Let me get some lunch together. How about salad and cold cuts? I have a delicious smoked ham and Thuringer in the icebox."

"Anything, anything at all."

That afternoon, as the two women sat on the front porch looking out to the lake and sipping their iced teas, they commented on the prettiness of the day. They talked of romance, they discussed flying and their plans for the future. Amelia spoke more freely, as if she were trying to make sense of her scrambled thoughts and unsettled life.

"When I was in Toronto, working at the military hospital, in 1917, I knew then and there that the only good thing about that god-awful war was flying. On weekends, you see, I would go out to the local airfield to watch the military aircraft taking off. I don't know why, but it just seemed as if the flying life would be an inevitability for me. But I really do not see how piloting is compatible with marriage." She paused, leaning back in her chair, and continued on with her musing as she adjusted her sunglasses. "There is a nice fellow, Sam Chapman, who was a lodger at my parents' home in California before they were divorced two years ago. He followed me to Boston. And he keeps asking me to marry him. But, truthfully, as much as I enjoy his company, I just can't do it. All I want to do is race the sky. Besides, what I have seen of matrimony has done little to inspire me."

"And why is that?" asked Lenora.

"Well, my father was an alcoholic. We pretty near lost everything because of him. And we were constantly moving. My poor mother suffered so. But, hey, don't get me wrong. I think a woman should have companionship. It's just that marriage with its medieval code of faithfulness does not appeal to me. How about you? Is there anyone special?"

Lenora grinned, as she gulped her tea. "There is no denying I have a sweet spot for Hanson. And he feels the same for me. But I hate to think that some man, however wonderful, will decide how I must live my life. Because it always comes down to that: men do ultimately influence a woman's self-expression. Besides, I have my work in Puerto Rico. I don't really feel that anything is missing. I'll have to see. But, look, let's take a swim. It is so humid, isn't it?"

Later that evening, Lenora and Amelia watched the fireworks extravaganza at Midway Park. The lake's entire rim had been outlined by flickering signal lights. Amelia had been impressed by the pageantry of the annual event and the Amusement Park itself, which had been festooned for the traditional July celebration with hanging lanterns and hundreds of little American flags. But best of all, better than their simple dinner of roasted frankfurters and french fries drenched in mustard, the wild rides, the large wooden bathing house, the toboggan slides that led into the water, had been, in Amelia's opinion, the glamorous indoor skating rink with windows overlooking stately steamboats at the Midway dock. She had kept repeating to Lenora, "Let's come back tomorrow night. I love to roller-skate."

PART SIX

TEN

AUTUMN 1927

LOVE FOR MILADY

Never had there been a time of such tranquillity and peace for Milady García de Demarest as there was for her during the autumn of 1927.

The love that Milady had received from her husband was the kind that, unawares, she had given him: particular and consistent. Whether it was ironing his jackets and shirts with detailed attention for hours, or making a special dinner that required full-day preparation, or making his office orderly, with its long shelves of multiple books and papers, folders and ledgers, Milady approached each task with equal devotion. Her husband's needs preoccupied her, just as hers filled him with wonder.

Each morning, as they sat down to a sumptuous breakfast, Henry Demarest would hold his wife's small hand and ask her about her plans for the day. On the rare occasion when she thought she might go into town for a bit of amusement, he would always reply encouragingly, "I think that's a splendid idea, my love. And why not buy yourself a pretty frock. Isn't there a dressmaker on Cristóbal Street?"

It was not enough for Demarest to share his material comforts with Milady; he sought to make his wife's world beautiful. And this he did in his own inimitable way. He delighted in surprises.

Knowing that she worried endlessly about her parents' welfare, he had decided to build a comfortable house for them. Clandestinely, he had sought the help of well-regarded architect, Antonín Nechodoma. Not telling anyone he had done so, he went about the necessary arrangements for construction of a modest yet distinctive house in *la sultana del oriente*, as Mayagüez was known.

When, one day, Demarest suggested that he and Milady take the train to her hometown to see how Los Señores García were getting on, Milady was delighted, but she could never have imagined the happiness she would feel that afternoon; the house that Henry had commissioned for her parents had been completed only days before.

Arm in arm, the couple strolled along a tree-lined street that led to Plaza Colón. Here and there they paused to look at birds and flowers. And, magically, a hummingbird alighted on Milady's sun hat. Henry stopped before the whitewashed dwelling. It was the first time he had seen the house himself, and he was pleased with the effect. "Who do you suppose lives there?" he asked his wife. And Milady, observing that the house was unusually designed, with its touches of rounded little windows, tiled niches, and fancy grillwork, answered, "I can't imagine, *amor*. But certainly, someone fortunate."

Finally, when they had reached the outskirts of the town and had walked to where the paved street met a narrow dirt road, they came upon a hovel of a cottage. Milady felt a sudden sadness. For ever since the 1918 San Fermín disaster, the home in which her parents lived was nothing more than a patched-up mess; its rusty tin roof open to the elements in more than one place.

Entering the derelict abode, Milady had fought back tears, all the while kissing and hugging her parents. Soon, Mrs. García brought out a pitcher of juice and a platter of syrup-oozing, fried plantains, but before anyone had touched the refreshments, Henry, dangling a key in the air, revealed his secret.

"*Señores García,*" he began, "Milady and I have, only moments ago, seen a remarkable house, which, I am pleased to say, opens to this large key. Would you like to take a walk with us to your new home?"

Milady would never forget that moment; how her father's jaw dropped and her mother almost fainted. No, she would never forget anything about that glorious, improbable instant, least of all the light upon her dear Enrique's face. Love overcame Milady then and there. An appreciation for his goodness that was so sweeping and over-whelming, it had frightened her.

Throughout their three-year marriage, Henry had given his young wife the attention of a man who understood the art of giving time. He would stop what he was doing, whether it was reading or working in the garden, to look into Milady's eyes whenever she spoke to him. It was not enough, for him, to listen to his spouse when she had something on her mind; he tried to comprehend his wife's concerns. He asked her many questions, often.

And there had been other, more amorous displays of affection. Intimate, small gestures, which, when pondered by Milady in quiet moments of the day, seemed significant.

Without her ever asking, Henry had begun an evening ritual that bestowed upon his wife a touch of ecstasy. He would give her an hour-long, luxurious foot massage.

Starting with her right foot, his fingers working in circular motion, he would press the little pads of flesh beneath each toe and, then, the creased recesses where the toes met the sole. This phase of the massage was just a prelude to more exquisite pleasures. The ritual progressed to more artful motions, and with them, slips of utter relaxation. Making a fist with his hand, Henry pressed the heart of each foot, first the right, then the left, kneading angry tendons, unraveling knots. With each new rolling motion of his fist, Milady surrendered something of her feminine control. Becoming happier, sensing liquidity in her neck, her chest, and the farthest reaches of her being.

LOVE FOR LENORA

Marriage to Milady had changed Henry's views on life in a number of ways, including matters mundane, such as his Sunday afternoon luncheons dedicated to political talk. To make Milady—who was not at all attuned to nor interested in the thorny issues plaguing Puerto Rico—more comfortable, he sought to make their Sunday afternoons less academic. Even if this meant having less vigorous, contentious discussions with Ignacio about the island's new governor, Horace M. Towner, whom Henry thought to be most decent and intelligent.

In effect, what had once been for him a much-enjoyed opportunity for debate with his young friend had now become a time of repose. For Lenora this altered pattern of the day presented new and awkward problems, as the situation encouraged Ignacio's increasingly daring *piropos*.

After they had eaten, Milady and Henry might excuse themselves for a siesta, and the responsibility of entertaining fell to Lenora. For Ignacio, these moments, sometimes hours, were like manna from heaven. He could go on endlessly with talk of her "long neck, sweet eyes, and golden hair."

It was true that Lenora had explained to him, on more than one occasion—most often when they took long rides on horseback—that she could not entertain a formal courtship. But he contented himself with thoughts of being able, some day, to persuade Lenora that a life alone was foolish, grim, and in Puerto Rico, especially, unacceptable for one so desirable and relatively young. Did she wish to be a spinster? Encouraged by the blessing of Señor Demarest in his pursuit of Lenora, Ignacio took any chance available to make sweet talk.

What Henry had felt obliged to exclude from their hour-long man-to-man conversation about his daughter's life, though, was any reference to her infatuation with George Hanson. For after she had gone to Hempstead Plains and had learned to fly, the aviation life and George were inextricably linked and always mentioned in any conversation having to do with her future. Nothing had prepared Henry Demarest for a daughter of so much spiritedness. For that matter, he couldn't think of any woman in his family, or in Louise's, who had exhibited such independence of thought and adventurous leanings.

Lenora had plainly disabused her father of any plans of matrimony with Ignacio with a speech about love, almost a manifesto of sorts. He could still recall what she had said, albeit with a few lapses and a few reactions of his own tossed in.

"Father," she had begun, "I am not now, nor have I ever been in love with Ignacio Portelli, although I do admit it might have been easier for all of us if fate had rearranged this situation. For what has happened is problematic, I agree. He tells me that I cause him pain, that I am stubborn. And you have made it clear you are fearful for my future and well-being. I, too, suffer, for I do not wish Ignacio ill. Nor do I wish you to worry. Can you not see that, for me, this is like an illness with no remedy? *Surely she did not mean that? Why this Puerto Rican man was exceptional in every way. He was charming, fine of character and physique. And learned.* If I turn against my soul, I will only be miserable. *Had she never thought about the joy of having children? And she wasn't all that young now. Twenty-seven.* To love, Father, is a different matter. I do not believe that love is something that one gives to or receives from another. Love is seeing the best in one's self and for whatever Godly reason, something or someone comes along who shows you this rare glimpse and you accept what has been shown to you. *Whatever on earth had happened to her? He didn't recognize his daughter.* Can you understand that love is just like that? It is, at long last, finding one's true self. And Ignacio, well, he is a decent man, a good man. It is true. But it is not Ignacio who has shown me who I am. It is George Hanson."

Ignacio also found some comfort in the notion that, sooner or later, Lenora would have to think of the future of the grapefruit farm. Surely, she must realize that her father, nearly sixty years of age, would not be able to manage the hacienda and plantation as he once had done. He was slowing down, anyone could see that. It was absolutely necessary that she marry, if only to take care of such practical matters.

But something else, more recently, had made him think his rationalizations were, perhaps, for nought. He had noticed that not once, during the entire year, since her most recent New York visit, had she adorned herself with the Florentine medallion she had always worn on Sundays. In its place was a brooch that he had never seen before: two wings of gold shaped as a heart.

THE FLAMBOYANT

To emphasize her independence, Lenora purchased her first plane that autumn, a single-engine Stinson, from an aviator whom she had met in San Juan, at an air show.

Noticing that Lenora had been examining the plane with more than just a little admiration, the owner of the ship, a Puerto Rican engineer, had asked her if she flew. And she had answered, "Why, yes, I do. But having a license without an engine does me little good."

The aviator was intrigued by Lenora, whose daintiness—pink silk dress and delicate jewelry—belied the strong, unrestrained spirit of a flyer. But she did speak without nonsense and directly.

"What do you call this bird?" she asked.

"*El Flamboyán.*"

"And why is that?"

"Its color. Like the tree. Don't you think?"

It was true. The plane was of a burning, orange-red, just like the island's ubiquitous flowering tree.

"Well, what would you say if I were to tell you I'm selling it? She's been a good machine. Dependable. Sound engine. But I'm interested in a bigger ship. The price is fair. If the answer is yes you will have to promise me one thing, though: you won't do anything as foolish as to try flying the Atlantic. I'm sure you've heard that just this summer a princess from England went down in a Fokker monoplane. Crazy old woman. Sixty-three. Thinking she could fly across *ese mar maldito*. Really crazy. Lindbergh may have been just lucky. Why, you know that nineteen pilots died this year alone trying to cross that ocean. Nineteen."

And so it was that Lenora came to find her very own plane, which she would call *The Flamboyant.*

But she would not make the promise she'd never try flying "that damnable water."

ELEVEN

SUMMER 1928

LONDON

Having made several inquiries of New York distributors with knowledge of the English citrus market, Lenora was certain enough about the success of the venture to plan a trip to Great Britain. In fact, what she had been told by a prominent grocer in New York was true: the British were, indeed, more partial to a slightly more bitter grapefruit than Americans. In early spring, she had written to fifteen of London's best hotels, arranging for appointments to meet with management about La Sardinera produce.

After a fairly uncomfortable crossing by ship via New York City, she found herself in London on a temperate summer's day. Walking along the Thames in the late hours of a June afternoon, Big Ben towering before her, Lenora took stock of all that she had done in a year, not least of which was purchasing *The Flamboyant* and building an airstrip behind the packing plant. She felt fulfilled and content. Excited about the future.

She had finally convinced her father there was nothing he could do to change her mind about Ignacio. And so Henry Demarest had channeled his energies into helping his daughter live the way she wished, even though it saddened him to see Lenora wander further from a path that, he felt, would have been more suitable for her.

Among the ways Henry Demarest showed Lenora that he supported her independence was to name her president of their grapefruit concern. Heaven knew that she had proven her abilities, time and again.

Lenora had just that morning come from Claridge's, one of London's finest hotels, and feeling jubilant about her successful meeting—the management, after consulting the head chef, had given Lenora a yearlong contract for La Sardinera citrus—she decided to relax and sight-see for the remainder of the day.

She had been to Trafalgar Square, the National Gallery, and Buckingham Palace. She had wandered about St. Martin-in-the-Fields, happening upon a majestically rendered organ recital. And, now, ambling along the river, she decided she would like to visit a shop in the vicinity of Westminster Abbey. Perhaps she would buy a piece of jewelry to celebrate the day's success.

Finding a cab, she rode to a boutique that had been highly recommended by the concierge of her hotel. It was, she determined quickly, a storefront that might have been very easily overlooked—so drab was the facade—were it not for its eye-catching knocker. She hesitated before she knocked three times, taking a good look at the object, a woman's hand, elegantly fashioned in bronze—the craftmanship was remarkable—complete with ruffled cuff and ring upon the index finger.

A middle-aged lady wearing a black skirt, black shoes with thick beige stockings, and a pale blue silk blouse, answered and greeted her with a crisp and friendly, "Good afternoon, miss. And how might I help you today?"

Lenora nodded as she answered, "Oh, I don't really know. Perhaps I'd like to take a look at rings."

"Yes, mmmm, I can help you there," the shopkeeper responded. "I have a case of truly lovely items."

Going to a long mahogany counter and kneeling down behind it, she brought out a display case in which there were arranged a variety of finger rings, jeweled and unjeweled.

Lenora looked at each column carefully and asked to see one ring whose stone she could not identify. "May I see that, please?" she asked, pointing to a shiny gold piece.

"Yes, yes, indeed. It's lovely, yes. Quite lovely that one. You see, the shank is covered in acanthus leaves. Twenty-four carat. Mmmm. And it has an interesting history. Shall I tell you about it?"

"Yes, please do," answered Lenora.

"Well, let us have a cup of tea, then. It is teatime, is it not? Yes, five o'clock." The woman gave to Lenora the ring, which she placed on her middle finger.

In a corner of the room, there was a small tea tray, on which rested an ornately tooled silver teapot, purple cloth napkins, and a plate of little sandwiches and cookies.

"Let us sit down. Over here."

The tea was delicious, clove-scented, the sandwiches plump with watercress and butter; the chocolate cookies delicate and thin.

And, so, relaxed and enjoying the opportunity to listen to a story,

Lenora sat back in her seat, and was treated to a tale about the famous Swedish opera singer, Christina Nilsson, an ardent Russian admirer, and a tourmaline token of affection.

THE FRIENDSHIP

*Ap*art from grapefruit business, there was another, perhaps more important, reason for Lenora's visit to Great Britain that early summer week. She had decided to be there for her friend Amelia on the occasion of her transatlantic crossing in a seaplane called *Friendship*. Lenora had no doubt that her friend would make the voyage without injury or accident. She would be the first woman to do so.

Amelia had, in strictest confidence, written to Lenora to advise her of the journey a month before. The three-engined Fokker would be piloted by the best: Wilmer Stultz and Louis Gordon. Mrs. Frederick E. Guest, an American who was married to an Englishman, had sponsored the flight. Although both Stultz and Gordon would be paid to undertake the crossing, Amelia was to go along without remuneration for "the fun of it, as a passenger only. I'll probably lie on my tummy, all the way, and look at the clouds. But, truthfully, I think I'm very lucky to be given the opportunity for such a grand adventure."

When the crew of the seaplane *Friendship*, after twenty hours, forty minutes, arrived in Southampton Harbor on June 18, Lenora, along with hundreds of other well-wishers, cheered wildly. The crew was boated ashore along with Mrs. Guest, and Amelia's life was instantly transformed.

Later that day, Lenora met Amelia at the venerable Selfridge's. At the invitation of the owner, Amelia was given free reign to take whatever she desired for her postflight wardrobe. The two women, delighting in each other's company, shopped all afternoon. It had been quite a while since they had enjoyed a good, long conversation and, finding that they had so much to catch up on, happily gossiped as each tried on evening wear. Amelia caught Lenora's attention when she mentioned that she had a secret: a new man had come into her life. Quite a bit older than herself. A New York executive. And while she didn't mention a name, and Lenora thought it inappropriate to ask, it seemed that Amelia, rather than seeking approval of this potential affair, was hoping to be dissuaded by her friend. "Is it wicked of me, Lenora?" she had asked. "He is married." And, then, looking at Lenora with wide eyes, she whispered, "Does it show poor judgment?" Lenora answering, "I certainly can't tell you what to do. But I am surprised."

"I know." Amelia sighed. "It is a bit shocking. Frankly, I didn't think there was a man on earth who would ever put up with the likes of me."

After trying on dress after dress that once-in-a-lifetime afternoon, Amelia chose three ensembles of velvet, silk, and satin in shades of champagne, turquoise, and pale brown. And Lenora, at Amelia's insistence, chose something for herself: a fancy red dress.

SEVILLE

While Amelia was adjusting to the glare of public life—being feted grandly in London, going to the theater and Parliament, Ascot, Buckingham Palace, teas and dinners at the invitation of lords and duchesses, royalty, and movie moguls—Lenora sailed on to the Iberian Peninsula. She was embarking on the trip for personal enjoyment as well as for edification. She had wanted to see the land of Don Quixote and Queen Isabella, figures she'd admired from her reading ever since she had been a child. She was also going with the purpose of buying a few items of Spanish furniture for La Sardinera.

Although her itinerary had included Barcelona, Toledo, and Madrid, her final destination was Seville.

When she arrived at the train station in that fabled whitewashed Andalusian city, a bit the worse for wear, disoriented and tired, she hired a carriage. The friendly young driver, happy to be speaking his native tongue to a foreigner, took her to a small, whitewashed *pensión*, owned by a courtly old man who walked with a limp.

Pleased that a pretty American woman, who spoke Spanish so well, had come to his establishment, the hotelier gave his finest suite of rooms to her: a small sitting room and bedroom, painted icy white, that gave on to a small courtyard, over which hung cascading boughs of red and brilliant pink geraniums. Such a flush of color that the walls seemed to exude flowers. A blue-and-white tiled fountain in the center played a ticklish music.

She had not eaten since early morning, and having mentioned this to Señor Vega, for that was the proprietor's name, he invited her to sit down in the communal dining room. Soon, the table was laid with small ceramic plates of food. There was sharp goat cheese, broken into little chunks, garlicky chips of sausage, potatoes oozing peppery golden oil, green olives, codfish fritters, and a loaf of country bread, heavy and hard-crusted.

Señor Vega poured two glasses of orange-flavored sangria. Then, he sat down next to the attractive American tourist and kept her company.

He was a loquacious character, eager to share tales about his beloved city and news about the imminent Seville exposition. He told his guest what sights to see—"la Giralda, first!"—where not to walk alone, and where to eat—Mesón Sol y Sombra should she wish to sample the city's finest cuisine.

After she had drunk her glass of wine punch and feasted on the various tapas, she went to her rooms to take a nap.

It was siesta time, when the city folded in upon itself from every corner, and all was silent.

She closed the heavy wooden shutters of her bedroom window. The room was dark, the tiled floors beneath her feet so cool. Then, she slipped out of her linen dress and took off her earrings. Feeling happy to be rid of clothing, she lay down on her fluffy, narrow bed.

She breathed deeply, inhaling all the potent scents of the mysterious place, something frying coming from the window of a nearby house, the scent of overripe lemons, and a flower essence, sweet and cloying like vanilla.

MESÓN SOL Y SOMBRA

At the suggestion of Señor Vega, Lenora went to dine at Mesón Sol y Sombra on the second evening of her stay. The restaurant, situated on a narrow cobbled street, was an old establishment, not too far from the *pensión*. It was owned by Señor Vega's cousin.

Having put on the frock that she had bought in London, a red silk dress with cinched waist and fitted sleeves, and a pair of high-heeled leather sandals that she had purchased on Calle de las Sierpes, she twirled around in front of the bedroom mirror, fanning herself with a gold-and-black silk *abanico*, and stomped her feet, making believe that she was a *dama sevillana* of the most illustrious lineage.

When she entered the little lobby of the pension, Señor Vega greeted her with *"Qué fina está esta noche, Señorita Demarest."* And, "Are you certain you do not wish to have me accompany you to the restaurant?"

"I'm just fine. Don't worry, Señor Vega. *Pero, gracias, gracias.*"

It was ten o'clock. A little early in the evening for *los sevillanos*, whose custom was to dine near midnight. But Lenora was famished after a long day's tour of the city.

As she walked the zigzaggy streets, a musty ancient smell like bergamet, alluring and romantic, surrounded her. This was the Spain of which she had dreamt, a land of arabesque secrets. The delicate Moorish architecture, its geometrical complexity, was meant, perhaps, to confound rather than illuminate. Lenora felt as if she were entering an ancient maze.

When she arrived at the *mesón*, she gave her name to the maître'd.

"Muy buenas noches. Señorita Demarest, we have been waiting for

you with great anticipation. Señor Vega told us you would grace our restaurant with your presence this evening. Please come this way. I have a very nice table for you. I think you will not be disappointed."

Lenora followed the man to a small room, nearly circular in shape, the last of three dining spaces. It was at the back of the restaurant. The alcove, whose walls were painted a sun-baked red and whose floor was paved in *azulejos*, brown and indigo, was redolent with the heady air of jasmine, for the room was open to a walled-in patio whose every inch was canopied with dark green foliage and its tiny star-shaped ivory flowers.

She sat down at her little table, placed a stiff napkin on her lap, and admired the decor. The room, bathed in candlelight, was a gift to the senses.

"May I take the liberty of suggesting some dishes?" asked her waiter. He was dressed in a white linen jacket, black bow tie and pants, his left arm covered with a starched linen cloth.

"Yes, please. But I do want to try your specialities. What the locals eat here, please."

"Of course. And to drink? Would you like to try a wine from our own vineyard?"

"Perfect."

The service was impeccable and prompt. Soon food and wine were on her table, and she began to eat. So seduced was Lenora by the romantic setting that she had failed to notice a young man who was sitting at another table, just a few feet away.

"Do you know what that is?" asked the Spaniard, as he peered over the top of his menu, pushing up his reading glasses.

"I am sorry," answered Lenora, as she turned to see the dark-featured young man smiling at her. "Did you ask me a question?"

The stranger smiled. "*Sí, sí.* I wonder if you know what you are eating?"

"Not really. I have asked my waiter to select for me." She laughed. "Why do you ask?"

"Well, it is not often, señorita, that a foreigner, *una americana*—you are *americana*, aren't you?" and Lenora nodded—like yourself chooses such a dish. You are eating what the locals eat at Mesón Sol y Sombra. In fact, in all of Sevilla, the delicacy is best prepared here."

"Well, what is it? What is this mysterious dish?"

"We call it *rabo de toro*. How do you say in English? I think, tail of bull."

Lenora swallowed, rolling her eyes. And then replied, "Well, tail of bull it is. And it is very good."

The Spaniard, thinking she was plucky and adorable, extended his left hand and introduced himself. "My name is Morales. Francisco Morales Ortega. *Encantado.*"

Within minutes, Francisco asked to join Lenora, and soon the two of them were devouring the savory foods that were brought to the table. There was fish baked in salt, with a spicy mayonnaise, *tortilla de patatas*, a mélange of artichokes and mushrooms drenched in oil, and crispy, garlic-fried prawns, among other succulent morsels.

When they had finally wiped each platter clean with bread, the waiter cleared their table. Dessert appeared, *tocino de cielo*, the color of burnt sugar, and two demitasse cups of thick, black coffee, its bitterness a perfect complement to the sweet, rich custard.

"Señorita Demarest, I should not be offended if you decline my request, but I would like to know if you would agree to hear some music, music that is ours, in Sevilla, this evening. Flamenco."

At that very moment, before Lenora had thought of how to respond to this impromptu invitation from a stranger, the owner of the restaurant approached their table.

"Señorita Demarest, *es un placer conocerla.* I see that you have met my son."

Lenora, raising her eyebrows at her dinner companion, answered, "And he is very nice." She extended her hand. The owner kissed it. "Thank you very much for such a delicious meal. *La comida es excelente. Excelente. Me gustó muchísimo.*"

Turning to Francisco and smiling, she added, "I have just been asked if I would like to hear a little flamenco."

"You are in safe hands, señorita. You can feel quite comfortable in Francisco's presence. And what is more, I think my cousin will breathe easier, knowing that his American guest has an escort this evening. He worries that a young woman, like yourself, roams alone in our city."

TRIANA

*I*t was midnight in Seville. Although she had always imagined
that the famous Andalusian city would be beautiful, she had not
imagined that it would be so lively. People, young and old, many of
them singing, walked arm in arm, along the major avenues, down ser-
pentine alleyways, and near the Parque María Luisa.

As Francisco and Lenora neared the newly built, El Alfonso XIII,
Francisco stopped.

"This hotel," he explained, "will be the pride of our city, I
believe, for years to come. The architect is José Espiau y Muñoz. It is
being constructed for the Ibero-American Exposition, Señorita
Lenora. Have you heard about next year's event?"

"Yes. Señor Vega has been a very informative host, I must say.
But tell me, Franciso, where are we going?"

"To Triana, the district of flamenco, on the other side of the river."

After they had crossed a bridge and walked down several dark
cobblestone streets, the lonely strains of guitar coming from windows and open doors, they came to a building where several men,
wearing tight black pants and high-heeled boots, their long dark hair
slicked back, were standing in a circle in front of the entrance. Francisco greeted them, and they in turn gave him a forceful hug. "¡Welcome, welcome, *hombre*! Paco is singing tonight."

They entered. In the darkness of the room, Lenora saw people
gathered around a wooden platform. It was exceptionally, almost
eerily quiet, and so she whispered to Francisco, "Can we sit down?"

He brought two chairs close to the stage and whispered back, "This, I think, you will enjoy."

It happened that the best flamenco *cantaor*, or singer, in Seville was in the little bar that evening. Lenora was about to witness a performance that would forever change the way she thought of song, for a "flamenco" used his voice as if it were an extension of virility. The voice of Paco, known as *El Fuego*, "The Fire," was the hoarsest wail, combining whispers, sighs, and ululations, sometimes rendering a dirge and sometimes a plaintive ballad. He cried, singing:

From your window to my window our street is so narrow . . .
As the interwining carnations kiss each other,
we imitate the flowers . . . Night and day we embrace.
That perfume, my love, I know not whether it is yours or the flowers . . .
Come to my kiosk . . . I have chestnuts from Gallarrosa, nuts and oranges
    from China, sweet potatoes and cinnamon drops,
melons from Konda all for my love.

Lenora leaned forward and dropped her head. She heard the thumping-against-wood of fingers on a guitar and then the razor-strumming of the instrument. Upon looking up, she saw that *El Fuego* was staring at her as he sang another tune. She felt her temples burn, her cheeks turn red.

My beautiful blond, listen to me without blushing . . .
I'm bleeding from the wound that you inflicted on me, my life, by your gaze . . .

Alas! . . . the little fallen tree no one notices . . . it is true that it gives
   no shade
. . . But when it was in flower that tree gave me blossoms . . .
a great many did I pick to present to my fair-haired love . . .
Now firewood is made from its dried-out limbs.

A dancer leapt onto the stage. A rumbling of staccato steps ensued.

I sit on my balcony all night, thinking of you,
and when I hear your footsteps approach, my heart fills with joy.
Why do I love you so much?

His body, like a blade, was desperate, sharp. An explosion. So frenzied was his dancing that Lenora felt its opposite effect. She became utterly still.

An adoring heart you shall have as long as I live . . .
an understanding love . . . eyes to weep for you . . . a man to defend you.

And then a tall woman, her shiny raven hair pulled into a thick knot, in ruffled, crimson skirt and fitted black blouse, walked slowly and deliberately toward *El Fuego*. One foot slowly put before the other. She raised her left arm high above her head and snapped her castanets against the forward flow of melody.

My love . . . this night and last, I waited for you. Where were you?
I did not know to whom I should pray . . . whether to your face
in the crowd or to the Virgin on the altar.

Come near, my beloved, I can no longer live
without you . . . You, having come into the world to torment
hearts, have pity on mine that is full of
illusions since I met you.

It was nearly three o'clock in the morning when Lenora got back to the *pensión* that night. Sheepishly she rang the bell, and soon she heard the uneven footsteps of Señor Vega coming to the door to let her in.

"*Y cómo te fue?*" he asked her. "Did you have an enjoyable evening, *guapa?*"

"*Sí, sí, Señor Vega.* I liked the restaurant very much. And later I even went to a flamenco bar in Triana."

Not feeling the need to explain further—besides, she thought, the owner of Mesón Sol y Sombra must have already informed the hotelkeeper that she had been accompanied by Francisco; everybody seemed to know each other's business in Seville—she excused herself, saying, "And now, I'm off to bed. I am quite tired, Señor Vega. *Buenas noches.*"

What he wouldn't have known was that Franciso, in a moment of Andalusian ardor, and no doubt encouraged by the indulgent quantities of brandy he had consumed that night, had momentarily lost control of himself on their way back to the pension. Grabbing Lenora at the waist, he had told her, groaning, "You are making me crazy. You are so beautiful." He had pushed her up against a white-washed wall—somewhere labyrinthine—and had begun to slather her face with kisses, until she had struggled to break free and walked back on her own.

TWELVE

AUTUMN 1928

RETURNING THE MEDALLION

*G*gnacio had been in particularly low spirits. The island's economy was sluggish. Sales of sugar were anything but robust; the market was getting tighter. The newspaper reports he had read worried him, too, as they indicated the United States was heading toward a recession. And he was feeling less than sanguine about his personal life. After more than ten very long years, he had been unable to persuade Lenora to marry him.

"A man your age," his father had said rather harshly that morning, while they were talking over coffee on the terrace, "has to think about the future. *¡Coño!* I'm an old man without grandchildren. If you had absolutely any sense, you would forget about this American woman and find a suitable, respectable Spanish bride."

The tense conversation was interrupted when Ignacio was called to the parlor by Zenobia, the housemaid. "A messenger," she announced, "with an important package" had just arrived.

Ignacio took the small wrapped parcel and went into the library.

Upon opening the box he saw that there was something wrapped inside, along with a neatly folded sheet of fine white paper. He opened the letter to read:

Querido Ignacio,

I trust that you are well and that your work is going smoothly in San Germán. As you most likely know, I was traveling in Spain over the summer. I walked the Ramblas in Barcelona, saw Goya and Velázquez in the Prado, toured the cathedral in Toledo, and while I was in Seville, I had a chance to buy some furniture for the hacienda. But I write to you about another matter, one that relates to you and me.

Perhaps you find it strange that I have never talked about the medallion that you gave me so soon after we first met. I was, to say the least, taken aback by such a rare and lovely gift.

From the moment I held the medallion in my hand, I knew it was unique. I read several books to ascertain its origin. And when I realized it was extremely valuable, a Renaissance gem, no less, I was even more touched by your generosity. And immensely flattered. And less than honest with myself.

I thought that I could accept such a present without allowing you the proper gratitude in kind. I mean to say, I thought it might be possible to accept such an object because you chose to give it to me.

Gradually, however, I understood that this was not true. When, at my father's wedding, you proposed, I knew differently, Ignacio. An adornment such as the medallion requires an owner of a deserving kind. A woman who can wear it as a token of your love.

And, so, I ask you to forgive me. Forgive the naïve girl I was; the woman I now am. Accept the return of this medallion, with my deepest

appreciation of your affection. And my heartfelt regret. Please let us,
always, dear Ignacio, be true friends.

A CRASH ON SAND

After Lenora had made a fairly miserable landing on the beach, she chastised herself for having been distracted by some troubling thoughts, including George's incipient controlling nature. She should have been focused on flying her plane.

Instead of concentrating on the land below her, she had been muttering under her breath about the ridiculous commentary she had read that very morning in the paper. An American banker had written a letter to the editor in which he suggested a solution to the problem of poverty in Puerto Rico. "Why not sell canaries to the peasants? They can teach the little birds to sing 'The Star-Spangled Banner.' Such singing birds would, I reckon, make interesting souvenirs for the growing American tourist trade." The arrogance and absurdity of such a theory greatly bothered her. And, then, this rumination, for some unfathomable reason, had led her to thinking about George Hanson's recent letter, a letter in which he had asked that she move back permanently to New York. "I love you, Lenora, and I'd like to take you as my bride. Just think: the two of us could fly around together. We could visit all the magnificent sights of the country and have a truly interesting future side by side."

While thinking all of this through, she had failed to see a grove of royal palms ahead of her. She had managed to take *The Flamboyant* down just in time, albeit crashing into one particularly huge tree. As a result, she appeared to have a broken rib. *The Flamboyant* had sustained a smashed landing gear, and one of its wings had cracked in half. Luckily she had been following the wide-open sandy beach, as George had recommended to her, with the warning, "Just be sure you follow the coast, at least until you get to know that Stinson better."

SAN FELIPE

*I*n the early morning of the thirteenth day of September 1928, as Lenora was riding through the fields, she noticed that the air was unusually heavy. At the same time, the coloration of the sky had abruptly turned charcoal and a fierce wind hit La Sardinera Bay.

Finding Pepe in the coconut grove, she yelled to him to warn the men and find his family, "Get them to shelter. La Casa Verde." Waving at the sky, she said, "Looks like a storm."

Riding on to the production plant, she told the packers to go directly to the school to get their children and insisted that they too run to the hospital for safety.

Then, she rode back to the house and with the help of Pepe began to prepare for the full thrust of whatever bad weather might come their way. "We must tie down the shutters," shouted Pepe. "*Puede ser un huracán.*"

Inside the house, Henry Demarest, following the foreman's instructions, cut heavy rope into twelve-foot lengths, and as he did, Milady ran around the house from room to room, locking the heavy wooden shades attached to all the windows and doorways.

Pepe and Lenora started on the second floor, quickly tying the shutters to pillars or, in the larger rooms, the concrete columns of the *mediopuntos*. By the time they had finished with the set of shutters in what had formerly been Milady's suite, but was now an office for Lenora, the rains were so heavy and the winds so strong, it was difficult to hear each other speak. Lenora motioned to her father and Milady to go to the storeroom, and after she and Pepe quickly put away as many loose objects as they could, they joined them.

When the hurricane unleashed its full force on La Sardinera, the group huddled close together. Milady began to pray aloud as the whistling, crashing, and ripping of trees and structures resounded. Two hours passed, the four of them imagining the horror outside, and after the final winds and crashing surf had quieted, a strange stillness followed.

Within days, news of the damage circulated throughout the island and Lenora learned how San Felipe had ravaged the terrain. It had come slowly from Cape Verde, striking Guadalupe with deliberate exactitude and, then, St. Kitts and onward. But the storm that hit the northeast coast of Puerto Rico on that morning was so fierce and unforeseen that the islanders had been totally unprepared for it. The hurricane had landed after dawn like a torrent of water on a small fire.

Eighteen-foot-high waves had hammered the coast with monumental power, hurling boats against the rocky cliffs of San Juan Harbor, killing fishermen with such indifference that their bodies and the bodies of their ships were rendered indistinguishable.

Later, they would all read the horrifying accounts in the papers; how in one small town several people, running for their lives, had been decapitated as their figures met the blade of tin roofs flying in the air; how in another village, a group of parishioners rushing to their church to pray were crushed to death when the chapel's new dome slipped from its mooring.

Towns had flooded in an instant, as the eyewall of the hurricane roared on. In the interior, vast coffee fields vanished. Farming communities completely disappeared. Bloated carcasses of animals and humans crisscrossed the countryside on rivers that had formed in seconds, sweeping out to sea. There were so many mud slides in the mountains that it seemed the mighty *cordillera* itself would collapse.

And for weeks the damage would continue, the aftermath of San Felipe bringing tragic consequences to many. Thousands of Puerto Ricans perished in flooded towns and many lost their homes and farms.

Such was the devastation that on the mainland Puerto Rico would be referred to as "the poorhouse of the Caribbean."

At the Demarest estate the only person who had been injured was Milady when she tripped on a massive ball of palm root and gashed her forehead on a rock. But other than this incident, none of the field hands nor any members of their families had been hurt, and for this, Lenora and Henry Demarest were immensely grateful.

Fortunately, the damage to the house and hospital was minimal thanks to the unusually thick cement walls and foundation of each, but the plantation had nearly been destroyed. Countless palms had been uprooted; many of the grapefruit fields had flooded. The packing plant had collapsed, and what remained of it looked useless. Worse still, the majority of laborers who farmed La Sardinera were homeless, their small straw huts reduced to mounds of refuse.

A few days after they had assessed the value of the damage to the estate, Lenora and Henry had a private meeting at which they discussed the future of the farm. "We should, I think, start trying to rebuild as soon as possible. If you agree, Lenora, perhaps we can begin next week. Get the men to clear the fields. And, somehow, we must find their families temporary shelter."

While Lenora thought that there was no alternative—after all the *finca* was important to them for so many reasons—the prospect of rebuilding daunted her.

And, then, one day, not too long after she had organized a team to lead the efforts, Lenora received a visit from Ignacio. He had come unannounced, and as she saw him ride up to the house, on horseback, she felt a crushing guilt.

Taking off his wide-brimmed hat, he waved at her and called out, "Lenora, I've come to help you and your father. We heard in San Germán, just yesterday. About the *finca*. All the damage."

What would he say next? she wondered. There was every reason to expect tension. And yet, here was Ignacio, ready to help as always. Willing to do the right thing, no matter the personal cost. This, of course, made her feel even worse about what had happened between them. He was, she knew, an exceptional man.

"Ignacio," she began, "I want to explain . . ."

"No. No. *Por favor.* Enough has been said already. It is neither your fault nor mine, Lenora. We must now live in the present, as it is. I am your father's friend, no? And I sincerely hope that I am yours. Here we are then, with a settled situation. So, please let me help."

And, so, Lenora made arrangements for Ignacio to stay at La Sardinera until he, with the help of Pepe, were able to make the first clearings in the grapefruit fields. And it was Ignacio who oversaw the building of temporary housing, simple barracklike structures made of wood and tin, until more permanent homes could be erected for the field hands who had lost their *bohíos.*

THIRTEEN

AUTUMN 1929

AGE

$\mathcal{L}$enora had just returned to Puerto Rico from Driftwood, where she had spent a week with George enjoying the fun rides on the Phoenix Wheel at Celeron Amusement Park; the late-night swims in Lake Chautauqua, twilight picnics; the excursion to Niagara Falls; the long hikes at Panama Rocks.

The realization that she felt more at home in Puerto Rico than in New York had heightened her awareness of the passing of time and of aging.

Just a few days before, upon her arrival at La Sardinera, she was struck by the feeble appearance of her father. He had aged considerably in a matter of months. Not only were his facial features those of someone older than he was in years—his auburn hair was evenly white, his jaws so thin—but his attitude of uncertainty had rendered him more fragile than she had ever thought imaginable. He had become a tentative man who questioned his ability to do the simplest of things. Gone was the wanderlust soul. The inquisitive warrior.

Gone too were the eagerness and gusto for newness of experience that had so marked his nature.

She was changing, too. What exactly did it mean to be a woman nearing thirty years, unmarried without children. Why was she not sad? And she was aware her face and figure were adapting to the weight of time, but wasn't bothered by that either. Milady, she supposed, was far more typical a woman of her age, as she fretted endlessly about emerging lines, especially those that framed her mouth—"like ridges on a seashell"—the occasional gray hair (could it really be!), the thickening at her waist. "But at least I am married," she would sometimes sigh when working in the kitchen, "married to the dearest man."

Flying *The Flamboyant* was a constant source of fulfillment and joy. Racing through the air, the sand and sea beneath her, revealed a never-ending liquid painting, an art of such splendor and changeability that it completely fascinated her.

It was on her escapades in air when thoughts of life and death were so sharp they took her breath away. It isn't that we age, she concluded, but rather that we disappear a bit each day, becoming finer and more delicate till our spirit becomes spirit complete, at the final moment of one's life.

She had explained this revelation to George, adding that the confinement of marriage left her unconvinced about the need to wed. "I have my work in Puerto Rico, I have flying, and we have each other's friendship, isn't that enough?" just as he had again proposed to her, out on the lawn near the bank of the lake, the two of them entangled in each other's arms.

And although she wouldn't tell a soul, including him, she had a greater dream than being someone's wife: she would some day fly the breadth of the Atlantic.

A PASSING

$\mathcal{I}$n the quiet of darkness, in the stillest moments of the early morning, a late October morning, while La Sardinera was at rest, Henry Demarest passed on. His death was as unassuming as the last breath of his life, fitting for a man whose ways were gentle, whose life had been devoted to the making of refinement.

Upon awakening that morning, Milady touched her husband's cheek and, in that second of intimacy, knew that he was gone. She did not weep at first, but rather, said a prayer, her arms around the man who had changed her life so greatly, who had shown her what it meant to freely give. Theirs had been a true love found, unexpectedly. Letting go of Henry, now trembling, tears running down her cheeks, she rushed to Lenora's room.

Upon being told of her father's death, Lenora slipped into her robe and went to him.

The first thing that she noticed was the sweet expression on her father's face, as if he had enjoyed a marvelous dream. And then she saw how exhausted he looked, his sunken cheeks, his crescent-lidded, puffy eyes. Her beloved father.

THE BALM OF MUSIC

At the funeral in Dorado's white colonial-style church, towns-people, laborers and farmhands, even strangers, as well as Henry's friends in San Juan were in attendance. Ignacio, who was heartbroken, gave a stirring eulogy for the man who had been, in many ways, more of a father to him than his own, even referring to the doctor as *"mi padre americano."*

Afterward, at the small reception for the family's invited guests at La Sardinera, Ignacio went to Lenora and asked to speak to her in private. Standing outside, near the ocean, the two of them nervously looking down at their feet, Ignacio made an offer.

"Lenora," he said, as he held her hand, "I want you to know that I am always here for you. No matter what, I am your friend, and always will be. If you need any help at all, for whatever reason, please, let me know."

Overcome with gratitude, she began to weep, and Ignacio, not being able to say another word, so pained was he at the thought of Lenora alone, embraced her tightly.

In the weeks that followed, Milady and Lenora grieved quite differently. Milady went about her day as if she were following a strict schedule, preparing breakfast, then making lunch, washing floors, polishing furniture, washing clothes and ironing. She spent countless hours ironing linens, absorbed in the meticulousness of making perfect creases in tablecloths and sheets, runners and handkerchiefs, towels, serviettes, as if trying to lose her thoughts in those many folds of cloth. When cooking dinner, she succumbed to bouts of weeping and, then, sought refuge in her bedroom, where she would draw for hours.

Lenora mourned apart. For days she did not eat; Milady's pleas "to have a bite" having no effect on her. She found it impossible to sleep.

Confusing ruminations—how could she not love Ignacio, a man who was so good, so kind, *what on God's earth was wrong with her;* her longing for George; her unadulterated grief—were met with the desire to make a life of meaning for herself. But lethargy prevented her from doing anything. Neither could she read, nor did she feel like riding. She could not find the will to make her daily rounds with Pepe. She did not wish to fly.

The only activity she engaged in was listening to recorded music, Granados in particular, as he had become her favorite composer.

She spent mornings, afternoons, and evenings pondering piano tunes. She had discovered the medicinal, healing properties of melody. The contagious rhythms of Granados's personality enfolded her. His music—reflecting *saudade,* "a sweet-sad longing"—more than anything else, far better than meditation, letters of condolence, or words of sympathy, provided her with some relief.

Sitting in her favorite reading chair, she closed her eyes and concentrated on the chords of grandeur, dulcet chords in pianissimo, in forte. Half-tone modulations of perfection. One exquisite composition followed by another.

A month went by like this, Milady and Lenora tending to their sorrows, sometimes finding comfort in each other's company, and just as often needing solitude.

It was during one of those nights of companionship, the two of them sharing a meal in the kitchen, that Milady told Lenora of her intentions. She had been reflecting for days on what she would do next, and had decided to return to Mayagüez. Henry had bequeathed her a considerable amount of money and the deed to her parents' house. "Lenora," she explained, "it isn't that I do not want to live at La Sardinera; rather, I think I should be living in the town of my birth, where I belong. My parents are alone, and I can be of help to them. Besides, this is your home. I thank you for the fortune, the most incredible fortune, of having found my love here and your good friendship. But time moves on. The good Lord wills it so."

The two of them hugged, knowing that Milady's words were spoken with a gentle wisdom.

STARTING OVER

After Milady left La Sardinera—the two women promising to keep in touch with frequent visits—Lenora thought long and hard about her options for the future. Henry Demarest had left his daughter a wealthy woman. In addition to owning Driftwood, she had inherited La Sardinera, more island acreage than she could possibly cultivate, commercial real estate in Jamestown, New York, and a healthy bank account.

In those first days of being absolutely alone in the house, she found that Pepe's kindness was a very welcome consolation. It was he who came to see if she had eaten breakfast, oftentimes bringing *desayuno* from his own home to her kitchen.

"Señorita Demarest," he would kindly plead, trying not to stare at her glittering blue necklace, "you must eat something. Here, please take this. Marianela has baked some bread and there is a bit of guava paste, too." Lenora found his quiet presence reassuring.

One morning, finding his young employer listless on the patio outside, the caring foreman asked to join her for a cup of coffee. Speaking softly, he began to tell a story.

The cadence and inflection of his Spanish was soothing to her ear.

"This is an old Taino myth," he began. "Long ago, before the world embraced the oceans and the sea, before the land knew water, there were four great mountains; one of which was called Borinquén or Land of Brave Men. One day, the greatest warrior on Borinquén went hunting for meat with his *tabonuco* bow when, suddenly, the earth turned angry and a rumbling of land demanded that the warrior put down his bow and arrows and follow the spirit force instead. When the hunter's family began to worry that their son had met an enemy, for he had not come home to them, the father went in search of his warrior son. The only thing he found was the *tabonuco* bow and arrows. He returned to his wife who, in her sadness, knew the time had come to give her husband a large gourd, hollowed out. The husband put the bow and arrows in it. He hung the gourd from the ceiling. The people, having lost their greatest warrior, went hungry for many days. And then one evening, the warrior's father took the gourd from the ceiling. Inside were many beautiful fish, enough to feed the people of Borinquén ..."

As Pepe wove his tale of days bygone, and then related others about Columbus and the Taino people, of great adversity and sadness and strength, Lenora began to feel, quite strangely, a glimmer of her old reliable self. Others before her had suffered. She was not alone.

That day led to another day of increased well-being, and eventually she resumed her daily chores. Routine in itself provided comfort and direction.

A QUESTIONNAIRE

Seven Puerto Rican intellectuals, many of them politicians, gathered in the airy parlor of La Sardinera on a Sunday afternoon. Though these men had gotten to know Henry Demarest far better than his daughter through the years, Lenora was determined to befriend these gentlemen whose ideas and philosophies her father had deemed as "worthy of consideration, right or wrong." The Puerto Rican politician, after all, was a rare individual; as capable of penning an accomplished sonnet as writing a compelling legal brief.

Although before her father's death Lenora had never felt inclined to discuss the U.S.–Puerto Rican tensions that, gradually, had escalated since the early twenties, she couldn't help but confront the frequent reporting of such difficulties in the local periodicals and newspapers. And with her father gone she assumed even more of a responsibility to help the people of the land she called her home. She felt it her duty to be better informed.

This Sunday afternoon gathering, she realized, was also an effort to stay close in some way to her father's habits and example.

The more immediate reason for the informal chat that afternoon was a questionnaire, which followed a series of essays written by Antonio S. Pedreira. It had been published in *Indice*, a periodical to which her father had subscribed, a journal whose purpose was to incite reflection among its readers on the legitimacy of American governance. And being moved by its intent, Lenora sought to be apprised of the matter by men who had dedicated their lives to answering the two-part question that was posed in the journal, specifically, "Is there a way of being indisputably and genuinely Puerto Rican? What are the defining marks of our collective character?"

"So," began Lenora, as she turned to Luis Lloréns Torres, a distinguished poet, sitting to her right, "how would you address these questions, Don Torres?"

The poet, momentarily lighting his pipe, nodded first toward his hostess and then toward the others present. He answered in the following manner, "*Pues, bien,* Señorita Demarest, may I first say that I think you are a most unusual American woman. You actually care, as did your father, about such matters. Who among your citizenry even knows what Puerto Rico is? From what I have read in your English papers, it seems the mainland thinks very little of our people. I must say that when our former governor, Mr. Towner, first came to our shores in 1923, I had great hopes for our island's progress. He seemed unusually sensitive to Puerto Rico's needs. But now I am absolutely convinced he had no intentions, whatsoever, of helping us in Washington. But, forgive me for straying. The issue of *Indice*. Yes, well, I would say that the *jíbaro*, the humble Puerto Rican countryman, the *jíbaro* is "the soul of our race."

And then the young political thinker Luis Muñoz Marín spoke to the question. "Our Puerto Rican nation is enslaved by American imperialism. The only way to truly be Puerto Rican is to be independent from a power that would keep us from our past, that would distort our present, and would tell us falsehoods about our future. I am and always will be *independista*."

Matienzo Cintrón, a politician, who was also present, began to cite from his poetic drama, *Grito de Lares*. What play had better underscored Puerto Rico's separatist view? After finishing, he added, "I can only say that Rodó's book *Ariel* speaks for all Latin Americans, including Puerto Ricans. We simply do not need the values of North America on our shores. We are a different race, formed of a different history, bleeding from the wound of 1898, a wound that will never heal, I tell you plainly, until we have self-rule. And I might add, we will never abandon "*lo profundo*," the soul of our culture, our language, no matter how intense the effort to educate us in English. Our children and our children's children and theirs will speak the language of our forebears. The Spanish language is our birthright, and we will not be robbed of it. Of this let there be no doubt. And need I remind any of you of how corrupted our language has already become by the intrusion of English? Just look at the official spelling of our dear island's name."

Next, a young poet among them explained what he believed to be the character of Puerto Rico. "The desire to live as music is made, freely, from the heart. The problem, my friends, is that we are orphans, without a country. We are not a nation. We are not a state. We are something entirely new. We are told by powers on the mainland that Puerto Rico is an 'unincorporated territory.' I ask you, what is that?"

Someone else discussed the overwhelming poverty in Puerto Rico. "Until we have an economy that works for all of us, determined by the historical, cultural, and sociological characteristics of our island, not those of the mainland, our countrymen will suffer greatly. And now, with the economic disaster in the U.S., what will happen to our fragile market? I suppose, however, we should be grateful for our new governor. This Theodore Roosevelt Jr. appears interesting. And he tries to communicate in Spanish."

Lenora listened with the utmost attention to these impassioned speakers. She was puzzled, though. She did not think they accurately understood America's intentions. And she was baffled by their reaction to improved schooling on the island, in particular, the efforts by American educators to teach English to Puerto Rican children. Wasn't this a positive endeavor for a country so poor? Was there really harm in teaching children several languages? She herself had benefited by being able to communicate in Spanish, so why not the reverse?

FLYING AROUND THE ISLAND

One morning in late November, Lenora got into *The Flamboyant* and headed south to Guánica Bay. The Sunday afternoon gatherings, which she had begun holding regularly, had inspired her to travel around the island. "If you really want to understand the way we think, see, experience reality as Puerto Ricans," said Luis Muñoz Marín, on one such recent occasion, "you must become familiar with our land, our people, not just San Juan or the fields surrounding your hacienda. You must study, Lenora, as your father studied, our history, geography, our culture."

As she steered her plane south, past el Río de la Plata, glistening like a slip of mercury below, she came to Vega Alta, then to Morovis, and farther down to Orocovis, toward Cerro Doña Juana. She was careful as she brought the plane up to a higher altitude and steady, making good time, as the wind was with the Stinson, she approached the Cordillera Central, that vast and rugged spine of mountainous terrain, where lay in veiny splendor hidden rooks and rills. This was the land of the *jíbaros*, as she remembered Llorens Torres telling her one day. "The countrymen who still live close to the earth, who are known for their generosity, their candor, and hardworking ways." Hidden in the mountain chain beneath her were countless coffee farms. Perhaps one day soon she would visit a few of them.

As she flew through banks of lamb-like clouds she was struck by the sunlight spinning off whiteness, sometimes flashing like a quickening blade, severe, and other times, diffused, a glimmering, like the light within a globe. Somewhere down below was Villalba.

Only thirty-five miles from the north coast to the south coast, the distance seemed longer with this high divide. But, soon, she left the treacherous peaks behind and found herself in a sky so blue the color hurt her eyes. Slightly tipping downward, she steered her bright red Stinson south and west toward the town of Ponce. She was getting closer now to Guánica. She lowered her altitude until she could see houses and trees, churches and farms and little squares, and soon she was over Ponce's beach and following the coast to Guánica Bay, the same bay, "where sixteen thousand American troops landed on our shores, July 25, 1898, without the slightest resistance from our people, on the contrary, to whoops of joy," as recounted to her by Muñoz Marín.

The bay looked beautiful, just like a painting by Georgia O'Keeffe, she thought. An interplay of earth and water, dark black, shadowy, with swaths of blue and white, the sea and spume, crisscrossed against the blind spots of the land.

She circled the bay again and again, tracing the lines of the coast, first narrow then wide and then narrow, again. Finally, having memorized the lay of terrain, she brought her wings up and headed farther west.

NOVEMBER TELEGRAM

Having poured herself a cup of coffee, Lenora walked out to the terrace on the second floor. The quiet shaded nook of the house had been her father's favorite place to read and think when he had wished to have some private time. Later, after he had married, he and Milady often breakfasted alone there. In recent months, Lenora had converted the terrace into something of an outdoor living room, Moroccan style, with carpets on the tiled floor, large urns of feathery fern and ruddy spadix, and comfortable furniture.

Finding Bendition resting on one of the large fan-back chairs, she sat in the other and opened up the telegram that Pepe had, just that morning, brought from town.

Five short sentences appeared as follows:

WISH TO MARRY IN THE EARLY NEW YEAR. SECOND WEEK IN JANUARY. I CAN COME TO PUERTO RICO. WAITING FOR REPLY.

LOVE, G. H.

Looking down at her crimson quilted slippers, she felt like the schoolgirl she had been when she first met George Hanson. Memories of him came rushing back to her. She remembered how he always touched his dimpled chin, an endearing mannerism, whenever he mentioned his plane, and how he held her right elbow, so lightly yet firm, when they strolled around the ship on that first voyage to San Juan. And she remembered their first kiss in Westfield, after she had gone up in the Oriole with him. His chapped lips upon her own, the feel of his cool, lean cheek against her face. After he had flown away to Buffalo, she had stood completely still, scared and happy, not feeling the cold in a field of Concord grapes, just thinking about that kiss. And she remembered how she wandered back to the square, along the fields, and continued past her Ford until she realized she was walking aimlessly, so elated was she by the revelation of his feeling for her. And there were other sweet moments of shared tenderness: in the train station upon her arrival at Hempstead; in a pretty sweet shop in the country on their way to his aunt Janet's house; in the hangar late one afternoon, when everyone had left and they were all alone; in a rowboat on Chautauqua Lake, and in the lake itself, the two of them skinny-dipping on a sweltering, cricket-orchestrated night in August. The night when they had seen a falling star and made love in the woods upon a mossy bank.

Bendition growled in his sleep and suddenly her reverie was broken. Looking at the telegram again, Lenora wondered how she should respond.

She put the telegram back in its envelope and walked to the railing to see why Jason, her dog, was barking so loudly. Seeing her good friend, Señor Iglesias, rather nervously shooing away the animal, she yelled out, "Do not worry, *no te preocupes*, he is a good dog. Just excitable, that's all. I'm coming Señor Iglesias. I'm coming."

IGLESIAS

I haven't seen you at the store in such a long time, dear, and I was wondering how you were faring all alone out here. I hope my visit isn't inconvenient."

Señor Iglesias stood straight as an arrow, his elegant, formal demeanor belying his warmth and wicked sense of humor. The old-fashioned Spaniard was, Lenora thought, an utterly charming gentleman; one of those rare human beings who, by virtue of their even, kindly disposition, brought sheer gladness to those in their presence.

"Well," Lenora sighed, "I thought it best to stay away from San Juan for a while. I haven't felt like traveling to the city much these days. And, heavens, your presence here is always welcome. Always, my friend. I miss you. I've missed you so very much. Let us go in. I'll make something to eat."

While the elderly jeweler roamed around the house admiring the furnishings, Lenora quickly arranged a sampling of leftovers together in the manner she had learned in Spain, a kind of tapas lunch. Never one to cook well, she had, at least, learned how to prepare a few simple dishes with Milady's instruction. She put out rice croquettes, fried yams, and coriander-flavored meatballs on the kitchen table for her guest, along with a pitcher of lemonade and some pineapple slices.

"Lenora," called out Iglesias, "the three paintings in the dining room, they are quite stunning. Who did them?"

"The two hanging side by side are by a woman named O'Keeffe," she answered, "Georgia O'Keeffe. And the one on the opposite wall is by an artist named Arthur Dove. I saw them at a little gallery. In New York. I'm glad you like them."

"*Sí, sí. Son, de veras, provocativas.*"

The two friends sat down, then, and began to talk about mutual acquaintances, the old Spaniard regaling his lovely young friend with the latest gossip from the capital.

"I hear Mansfield wants to return to the mainland," began Iglesias, pausing for effect, before continuing, "but it seems that he got poor Adelia pregnant, you remember her, his office girl. And, now, he'll have no other choice but to marry the young woman. She told me she'll never go to the States, never. So, I imagine he is here to stay."

"I'm glad for that. I need him more than ever, now. Mansfield, despite his being somewhat of a Don Juan, is very reliable, a savvy businessman. He has been a boon to the company. Our shipments are always sent on time. Well, I guess I should thank Adelia for keeping him here." She winked at her guest.

"Tell me," said Inglesias, leaning closer to Lenora, "whatever happened to that fine young suitor of yours, what was his name, Ignacio, isn't that right?"

"Oh, Señor Iglesias, it is a long and tiresome story, I am afraid."

"Well, then, tell me of your flying. Is the experience really as extraordinary as you aviators would have us believe?"

"Oh, yes," answered Lenora. "There is nothing to which I can compare the feeling, nothing at all. Flying has changed my life." Lenora patted Iglesias on the back, adding, "But why not go to the patio for tea. I've got a lovely tin of pastries. And we can chat there."

That leisurely afternoon, Iglesias and Lenora talked about the world of aviation and Lenora's growing fascination with the sky. And while she hadn't minded much her solitary days at La Sardinera, it was, she thought, so nice to have intelligent companionship. Iglesias never seemed to have a care in the world. He was attuned to beauty. He saw splendor in everything, whether it was the way the wind moved leaves and flower petals, or the oscillation of the ocean, the simple yet exquisite form of broken coral thrown up on the beach, the shape of someone's eyes, or the sound of chimes, tingling in the breeze. The design of the smallest things did not escape his observation.

That afternoon, as was his custom, he gave Lenora a sampling of books he thought she might enjoy. And he had brought along a little something else for her, a gift: an unusual bracelet. "For your amusement."

As he took the piece of jewelry from a leather box, he said, "Come closer. I want to point out certain details about this piece that, I believe, are simply"—and he paused, his voice becoming quiet—"extraordinary."

The jeweler held what appeared to be a sort of charm bracelet with all the tiny objects made of porcelain. The chain from which the delicate charms were hung was of a rosy, intricately woven gold. "Obviously, this band must have been especially ordered, as there are many references to a personal life. Here. This charm"—and the little object he was referring to was an open book—"has painted on it the names of a woman and a man, connected by a love knot. And this little lute, it has a secret chamber. Look: inside is a ruby heart. The fan actually unfolds as well. Go ahead, just move the parts from left to right." Lenora did as she was told and saw the pretty marvel. Opened fully, the diminutive fan had painted on it an oriental scene, a plum tree in bloom and a peacock in shades of aubergine purple and green. "Now, what is truly extraordinary, in my opinion, is the next little bijou." Lenora saw he was pointing to a miniature white box on which was painted tiny golden flowers. "It is a jewelry case." Iglesias smiled broadly. "Let us look inside." As he flipped open the tiny latch, the interior, painted dark royal blue, was revealed. There were lilliputian gems—a diamond pin, an emerald ring, and the smallest pearl necklace imaginable—resting within.

"I came upon this remarkable bracelet in Holland of this year, when I was visiting Amsterdam. I am quite certain it was made in Meissen, Germany. The delicacy and luster of the porcelain is quite unmistakable. Mid-eighteenth century. Anyway, my dear, it's yours, this band. I wanted you to have it, at this most difficult time in your life. Hopefully, you'll always remember your old friend Iglesias when you chance to wear it."

FOURTEEN

WINTER 1929

THE GREEN HOUSE

The small green clinic, known to the people of Dorado as La Casa Verde, had been neglected by Lenora, following her father's death. There had been so many matters to consider, so many business and personal interests demanding her attention, that she had forgotten about the little hospital's administration.

One day a certain Ana Domínguez, the nurse who had helped Henry with his practice, came to the house.

From the kitchen, where Lenora was cleaning, she heard an insistent knocking and then the high-pitched timbre of the doorbell. She put down her mop and walked to the entry way.

"*Muy buenos días,* Señorita Demarest," began the woman, as Lenora opened the heavy oak door, "I am so sorry to bother you, but I thought it would benefit all concerned if I were to apprise you of the goings-on at the clinic." Without pausing, she rambled on. "There are, as you know, many people, employees of La Sardinera as well as townspeople, who come for treatment at La Casa Verde. But since the death of *su papá,* I have been left without the proper medicines.

We have almost nothing in our cabinets. Señorita Demarest, I do not know what to do."

"Please come in, Señora Domínguez. We can talk about this on the patio." The nurse looked nervously around and asked, "Is that leopard here?"

"No. Please do not worry. Bendition wouldn't hurt a soul, I promise you. And, anyway, she is resting in another part of the house." She pointed above her head. "Upstairs."

The two women settled into their chairs, and no sooner had they done so, than the Puerto Rican nurse continued on with her agitated plea.

"As I was saying, Señorita Demarest, we need to do something about the clinic. Your father was exceptionally organized. Exceptionally organized. He managed the clinic very well, and when it came to ordering the various pills and medications that are needed for our patients, well, he was fastidious. We were always well stocked at La Casa Verde, Señorita Demarest. You see, we have field hands coming in quite regularly. They need salves and liniments. Some of the poorer people in Dorado come to us with hookworm. A few have tuberculosis. There have been several cases of bubonic plague. And we have quite a few male patients seeking relief from, well, I suppose I should be blunt about it, venereal disease. Syphilis, particularly. Pregnant women are our patients too. And children and the elderly need regular checkups. What am I supposed to do, Señorita Demarest? Have you thought of finding someone to take your father's place?"

"Señora Domínguez, forgive me for having been so remiss. What with so many responsibilities here at the plantation and personal adjustments, these days, I guess I simply forgot about the clinic's adminstration. I am so sorry. But, yes, of course we must look for another doctor. And the medications that you need. Perhaps I can fly to San Juan to get them, let's say, tomorrow or the next day. How would that be?"

"Anything, anything at all would be an improvement. I can give you a list of supplies. I suppose I can tend to the patients myself until another doctor can be found. Thank you very much. Well, I must be on my way. I have a two o'clock appointment."

The nurse rose from her chair and hurried to the front door of the house, Lenora following after her.

"Don't worry, I will do whatever I can to help you. I will travel to San Juan tomorrow, but I'll need the list."

"*Sí, sí*, you will have it by the end of the day. *Adios, adios. Y gracias de nuevo.*" And off ran Ana Domínguez, trying to pin a small white nurse's cap to her unruly thick black hair as she headed toward La Casa Verde.

Lenora returned to the kitchen to finish her cleaning. Then, she went to her study.

She began to tackle the thick pile of business correspondence, letters from Europe and orders from various vendors in New York State and Pennsylvania. In general, La Sardinera business was quite good, as she had been able to acquire new markets in American towns other than New York City, places such as Elmira, Erie, Saratoga Springs and Albany, in addition to several small villages in Long Island, thanks to Janet Rowan's help. And, in more recent months,

Pittsburgh and Cleveland. She had also received positive word from three hotels at Chautauqua Lake; one hotelier taking the time to write a touching postscript at the bottom of a formal business letter: "We would be delighted to serve citrus grown on a plantation owned and operated by one of Chautauqua County's daughters."

Having answered an assortment of inquiries regarding the price and availability of La Sardinera produce, Lenora turned to another pile of correspondence, related to more private matters. There were letters from Amelia Earhart, in which she sought advice about a persistent suitor, a publisher in New York named George Putnam; letters from Janet Rowan; postcards from Milady, and some *tarjetas* from her friends in Seville. And there was the telegram from George.

She read and reread George's short, yet insistent, message. A wedding in January. In Puerto Rico. No, she did not want to lose George Hanson. But to abandon her life in Puerto Rico? Was it possible, she wondered, to be in love yet wish to live alone?

Taking out her best white stationery, she began to write a letter in response. But rather than answer George directly, she proposed an idea she hoped he might consider. Would he come to Puerto Rico for the new year? "Dearest George," she wrote, "I can't imagine a more splendid way to ring in 1930 than to have you with me at La Sardinera."

A PLEASANT AFTERNOON

After Lenora landed at an airstrip very near the train station in Mayagüez, she took off her leather flying cap, brushed her hair, and applied a little makeup to her windburned face. Although she wasn't particularly vain, she did wish to make a good impression that afternoon, and so she had brought along a change of clothing, a navy skirt and a lacy blouse, and a pair of comfortable leather shoes.

She briskly walked to the hangar, found the manager, and asked if she could keep her plane on the premises for the day. The manager, delighted to oblige the pretty aviatrix, was extremely surprised to know that a woman flyer lived on the island.

"I have never heard of you," he said to Lenora, quite incredulously. "I think it extraordinary that you fly."

"And why is that, señor?"

"Well, you are a woman."

"Women do fly, Señor, Señor . . ."

"Rivas."

"Señor Rivas," and she smiled slyly. "Women do fly all over the world."

Without futher comment, she went to find a place in which to change her clothes. Then, she asked one of the mechanics for directions to Plaza Colón.

She had never been to the southwestern part of the island and immediately became aware of the difference in climate. It was less humid than it was along the north coast. It was also very lush, as the Caribbean Sea nourished the landscape's tropicality.

As she walked along, she observed the remarkable architecture. New homes painted white and dusty rose, most of them grand, had been built on several wide avenues.

Milady had written the week before to ask if Lenora would come and visit. Los Señores García had wanted, in their own way, to do something for the woman who had changed their circumstances for, in truth, it wasn't Henry as much as Lenora who had altered the course of their lives. She had employed their daughter, at a moment when it looked as though they would be forever destitute. Of course, Henry Demarest had been something of a *mago*, too. His generosity, never failing.

They did not *know* Lenora Demarest. They had met her at their daughter's wedding, but, in Puerto Rican fashion, they believed that all of them were family, and they should become better acquainted.

It was thus that Lenora, having received Milady's letter, decided to fly to Mayagüez to spend an afternoon with the elderly couple in their "beautiful new home."

The first thing that Lenora noticed as she approached the white cement house with ceramic-tiled roof was that it lay close to the street, but was framed by two silk cotton trees. The house was gated with grillwork shaped like intertwining violins.

She rang the bell and soon heard heavy footsteps coming toward her. It was Señor García who opened the door, with a friendly, enthusiastic welcome. "*Tanto tiempo, tanto tiempo, hija. Muy bienvenida.* Milady and her mother are in the kitchen preparing something spectacular for us to eat. Please come in."

Lenora followed her host into the parlor of the house, which was decorated simply. They walked through a small alcove that led to an interior patio full of birdcages—the song of canaries, a mellifluous greeting—one avocado tree, and red ceramic urns of flowers and then into a short hallway that brought them to a kitchen in the back.

Milady, who was bent over the table, looked up to see her friend and rushed to hug her.

"Lenora, *qué gusto verte amiga*. I am so happy to see you."

Then, Señora García embraced Lenora, saying, "Why have you not come sooner? We have wanted, so very much, to have you visit, spend some time with us. Well, the important thing is that you're finally here."

"We are making *pasteles*, Lenora," said Milady, winking. I think they are your favorite, no?" And, then, "What can I offer you to drink? Would you like some juice or coffee? Or, better yet, *papá*, why not give Lenora a glass of your famous punch?"

Lenora, taking a small glass of the *ponche*, rich with cream and rum, topped with a sprinkling of cinnamon and nutmeg, went with Señor García to the patio, where the two talked about the Demarest plantation, farming in general, and the economic situation in the western part of the island.

"As you know," began the elder man, "we lost everything with the hurricane of San Fermín. But, Milady's inheritance has saved us. Milady is a good daughter, attentive and sweet, as I'm sure you know very well. We are living comfortably and, what is more important, happily. I do not think that Americans comprehend this notion. *La familia*, Lenora, that is what matters *lo más importante* in this life on earth. And faith in God." Taking a sip of his punch, he closed his eyes and smiled broadly. "*Qué bueno, no?*" And, then, staring at his guest, and rubbing his right temple, he nearly whispered, "My daughter tells me that you own a flying machine. How incredible. You are a courageous woman. She told me that you have named this machine *El Flamboyán*. Did you know there is a poem, a beautiful poem by one of our poets, with that title? Let's see. How does it go? Yes, it is like this:

> *"Sensual torch that warms and brightens*
> *in violence the plains and mountains*
> *fountain of blood, marvelous crest*
> *in your ardor summer rests*
>
> *"The fire flower in your crown humbles*
> *the Caribbean light in which you bathe*
> *amd the Antillean landscape bows*
> *before your luminosity, made honey from the cane.*
>
> *"From your sparkling ruby jewels*
> *purple in flame the horizon cleaves*
> *crystals red in insolations*
>
> *And between the sky and earth surprised*
> *by tropical foliage set ablaze*
> *the rebellion of hearts enslaved."*

Señor García's tempered voice relaxed and hypnotized her. As the old man and the young American were pondering the majesty of nature, Milady called out, "Lunch is served."

Afterward, when the dishes had been cleared away, the family took Lenora to the garden. There, amid the fleshy blooms of *gliricidas*, they talked for hours; Señor García returning again and again to the subject of the land's fertility. "So many things grow well here. Sugarcane, coffee, cacao, cotton, rice, corn, mangoes, mangoes, mangoes," he boasted. "And speaking of mangoes, how about a little dessert? Milady has made her special mango flan for this occasion, just for you."

And when Milady extended an invitation to spend *La Navidad* with the family, Señora García commanded that it be so, adding, "You must spend Christmas Day with us. You must."

By the time Lenora was ready to depart, it seemed that the entire community of Mayagüez had heard the news: that among them there was a "flying lady." At the airstrip, a large, curious crowd had gathered around Lenora's Stinson, touching the wings, peering into the cockpit, trying to find evidence that a woman, indeed, owned the brilliantly painted plane. As Lenora strode toward them, somewhat amused by the cheering, she saw a little girl who reminded her of Rosita. She lifted the child up to get a look inside.

When she finally climbed into *The Flamboyant* and opened the throttle, the crowd moved back. Lenora sped ahead, down the dusty runway path, and in an instant she was apart from them, high, and leaning toward space. And in farewell, the red ship circled twice, before it disappeared. Just as if a flame had been extinguished by the sea.

REMEMBERING CHRISTMAS PAST

A few days before Christmas Eve, Lenora handed out to her employees Christmas gifts of Belgian chocolates, rum, and *turrón*, as well as Spanish hams, serranos, and thick, fatty bacons. For Pepe, she had added yet another gift, a generous sum of money so that he and Marianela might buy the nicest Three Kings Day presents for their children.

After everyone had gone home for the day, she rode back to the house. She prepared a *merienda* of a sandwich, and went out to the patio to eat it, while she looked through her mail. Seeing a Christmas card with George's return address, she put it on the top of the pile.

Looking out at the ocean, the warmth of the sun upon her shoulders, she found herself remembering what Chautauqua County looked like in December. She remembered the drifts of powder snow that raced across the fields and lanes, the iced-over trees, and the icicles that decorated their house when she was young, huge daggers of crystal dripping from the edge of the roof, in front of her bedroom window, and the cracking, snapping when the weight became too great to bear and they would crash against the panes. She remembered walking in the silent, darkened woods, past rows of fastigiate trees, bare and solemn, and watching deer in their pursuit of tender buds for food, how quietly she would move until she got quite close, close enough to smell their feral odor, sharp and stinging in the bitter air. She and the deer standing deep in snow, exchanging shy glances. Sometimes she would lie down on the forest floor and make angels, waving her arms and legs back and forth, until the fanning of her arms and legs became the widest of heavenly wings. How carefully, so as not to ruin the pattern, she got up from her silhouette.

It had been so many years since she had been able to experience the stark beauty of a snowy winter. And the bliss of skating on Chautauqua Lake. She recalled how her father and mother, standing on the snowy banks, had shouted out to her, "Don't go too far, darling." Gliding close to shore, her private, magnificent ice rink, she would imagine that she was a ballerina or one of the seraphic visions she had seen in paintings, their hair dripping with seaweed and frost, glittering with stardust.

With the crashing of waves against the surf, her reverie was interrupted and she began to sort through the envelopes before her. She picked up George's card.

"Darling," he had written,

I cannot wait to see you. And, yes, I'll come for New Year's Eve, of course, I'll come. It will give us time to talk about the wedding, which will be small, won't it? I've been thinking too about our living arrangements. Perhaps it would be best if I stayed with you for a time in Puerto Rico. We won't have to go back to New York until, let's say, the spring. Long enough for you to settle your affairs. I don't know, darling, how you manage all alone, there. It seems a terrible burden. Well, we can talk about this when I arrive, which will be, by the way, on the twenty-ninth. I should be there at noon, or thereabouts. Lenora, dearest, I'll be dreaming of you, sending kisses on the twenty-fifth of December. Merry Christmas, my love!

Yours forever, G. H.

GETTING READY

*H*aving spent the better part of an enjoyable Christmas Day with Milady and her parents and some of their friends in Mayagüez—there had been singing and dancing, games and a skit—Lenora had been happy to fly back to Dorado the following morning.

She had adjusted, in truth, better than she could have imagined to the cast of her new life. And she had, finally, at the insistence of Pepe, hired a live-in housekeeper, a widow named Petrona Perez, a practical woman with a penchant for home decorating. No sooner had Petrona come to La Sardinera for her interview than she began to reorganize the house, suggesting that the kitchen be remodeled to allow for more storage space, the furniture moved around, new flowers planted. Lenora liked her pragmatic, approach to solving everyday annoyances. For instance, the persistent invasion of birds in the house. Honey-creepers had been flying in the kitchen for as long as Lenora could remember. When Petrona, upon entering *la casa* for the first time, had seen the kitchen-turned-aviary, she had exclaimed, "*Esas reinitas no deben estar en la cocina, no, no.* Of course, it is possibly your fault that they are here. You've got a bowl of sugar on the table. There is no better way of attracting 'little queens.' They'll violate any boundary if they get a whiff. You should put sweet trimmings in the cupboard."

On that lovely, clear morning in December, Petrona, dressed in a simple blue dress and emitting the scent of gardenia everywhere she went, served a sumptuous lunch of yucca, shrimp, and pepper casserole and a salad of tomato, corn, and onion. The delicious repast was set out on the patio, along with huge pots of poinsettia for decoration. And there was a bottle of champagne, "in case you wish to have a little cheer."

Lenora invited her housekeeper to sit with her and share the meal.

"Petrona," she began, as she poured two glasses of the sparkling wine, "a visitor is coming to stay for a while, a gentleman from America. He is arriving in four days. Could you prepare the guest bedroom?"

"Whatever you wish, Señorita Lenora. And what is this gentleman's name?"

"Señor Hanson. But you can call him Señor George."

"*Muy bien.*"

"Another thing, Petrona. I would like to have a party New Year's Eve, for the workers. Something festive. Do you know where I might purchase paper lanterns and fireworks?"

"*Sí, sí, Señorita Lenora.* There is a place in town, a little store behind the church. They sell religious statuary, candles, and *la pirotécnica de España.*"

"Good. Maybe we can go together to this shop tomorrow. As for the food, I think a buffet. You can make whatever you like, as long as there is enough for a hundred. I imagine there will be more drinking than eating. Still, we need to have a lot of food. Plenty of rice and beans. Maybe paella with chicken. Fruit. And pastries. However many assistants you need, I can hire for you."

"Señorita Lenora, if I may, I'll ask my nieces, the daughters of my brother, to help me. They are very hardworking. And as far as the food, do not worry about the particulars. I'll do something *muy típico.* A party this large requires *lechón.* You do know *lechón, no?*"

"Of course, Petrona. Whatever you say. You make up the menu."

The two women, then, ate silently, all the while thinking their own thoughts.

ARRIVAL

Owing to particularly stormy weather, endless squalls, and rough sea that last week in December, Lenora had been informed by Jonathan Mansfield that ships were coming in one and two days late to San Juan Harbor. No doubt, he surmised, that would mean George Hanson's ship would be delayed as well.

As it turned out, the White Star ocean liner on which George had sailed did not arrive on January 29, as scheduled. Lenora had flown out to San Juan only to spend the entire day waiting anxiously. On the morning of January 30, she flew again to the capital, hoping that George would be at port. Around her neck she wore a rosary that Petrona had given her.

George was standing on the quayside, just below the old town, holding a large bouquet of multicolored carnations and waving as Lenora, dressed in jodhpurs and a black silk blouse, ran toward him. The two embraced, kissed, and embraced again.

"I do not want to let you go, Lenora," he murmured. "Darling, you smell so good. My God, what a crossing we had. I am grateful to be on land."

Had he noticed that her face was thinner than it used to be? That there appeared around her eyes the lines that come from mourning? Had he noticed that her hair was longer, a bit darker? Or that she seemed more buxom? Lenora wondered if George Hanson cared that she had changed since last he saw her.

As they flew from San Juan's airstrip to La Sardinera, George kept staring at the woman at his side—and she was a woman. Gone were the giggles, the wide-eyed expressions of amazement, the childish clothes—what had she been wearing when he had first lain eyes on her, could it have been a navy pinafore of some sort—and the smooth face, the full cheeks. She had been an unusually pretty girl. And something about her spirit, he had seen right away, was out of the ordinary; artistic *and* level-headed. Since their most recent time together at Chautauqua, she had matured to even more pleasing effect. He liked her curvier figure. She was good-looking still. He watched Lenora as she calmly and efficiently steered west and took them through a wall of cloud. Suddenly they were in a brilliant cadmium sky, clear for miles.

"It is so wonderful to be back here. And with you. This is the happiest I've been in a long time."

Lenora smiled as she quickly touched his hand with her right hand.

"Look left. See that river?" she shouted above the droning of the engine. "When the hurricane struck the island a year ago, it was so flooded it destroyed three towns. Nearly four thousand people lost their lives, George. It was horrific." And then lowering her altitude, she said, "We're almost there, now."

Tilting left and gliding downward, they went inland, just past the coastline. Below them were green fields and little huts in clusters. "So many people live like that, in those little flimsy hovels. They are incredibly poor. But truly, George, there is a gentleness of spirit in this land that I don't think exists back home."

Keeping the Stinson on a steady course, she and her love were now flying over rolling hills, dark green oscillating swaths of vegetation with shades of watery green, raked deep with fertile red.

George saw an airstrip to his right.

"That's mine," said Lenora. Did he detect a glint in her eye? "We're going down."

EXCHANGING PRESENTS

When Lenora walked though the heavy wooden door into the entry, with George close behind her, it seemed as if she had walked into a stranger's house. She hardly recognized the spacious parlor, so changed did it appear with Petrona's artistic flourishes.

Small white candles flickered in every corner with terra-cotta urns of pink, red, and white poinsettia placed throughout. A fig tree displayed gold and silver Christmas ornaments, brought back from the mainland. And the furniture in the sitting room had been rearranged to allow for intimate discussion. Petrona had placed pillows, in deep shades of turqouise and green, on the chairs and sofas.

"Buenas noches, Señorita Lenora," greeted the housekeeper. *"Buenas noches, Señor George.* Your dinner is in the dining room. I do hope the two of you are hungry. And, Señorita Lenora, if you need me, I'll be

in my room. As tomorrow is a big day for us all, I wanted to get up early to begin my work, so I thought I'd retire early tonight."

"Fine, Petrona." And, then, Lenora waving her arm around her, added, "Thank you for everything. The house looks so festive."

George Hanson, looking high and low, whistled his approval.

"Wow, what a place you have here."

"Why don't you take a walk around, while I change,"she replied. "Oh, and if you want to take a shower, your room and bath are on the second floor, two doors to your left at the top of the stairs."

Lenora disappeared and George began to wander. From the large tiled front hall he strode to the far wall of the living room. A light breeze wafted through the open windows, filling the air with the delicate scent of bougainvillea. The room was a blend of American casual and Spanish high style. The stucco walls, painted a dusky tangerine, were offset by the ornately tiled floors. He had never seen such floors, indigo and pink and green in complicated, geometric design. Peering through the opened stained-glass windows he could see the ocean, wide swaths of ivory foam cresting on glassy aquamarine.

He stared out the window, watching the setting sun disappear beyond the horizon.

After a few minutes of reflection, he slowly walked up the broad, open-arm tiled staircase and went to his room.

When he passed through the door, he saw that much attention had been given to his comfort. On the desk before a window, there were a pile of paper, pens and sharpened pencils, some maps of Puerto Rico and nearby islands, a jug of water, and a platter of unrec-

ognizable yellow fruit, whose scent was a blend of banana and rasp-
berry. A large bouquet of tiny blue flowers rested on the dresser. And
in his closet, lime-scented, fluffy white towels, a navy cotton robe,
and a pair of men's leather slippers.

After taking a long, hot shower, he shaved and patted himself
with a light pine-scented cologne. Then he put on a pair of white cotton trousers, a light blue shirt, and a loose-fitting beige linen jacket.

As he entered the dining room, he heard soft music, the strains of
a guitar coming from the gramophone. Before him was a table laden
with fish, rice salad, red beans, cheese and rolls, as well as tall, silver can-
dlesticks of varying shapes. There stood Lenora, lighting the candles.

"You must be famished," said Lenora. "But would you like a
cocktail first? I've got rum and whiskey. And a good Spanish wine."

"How about something strong."

As she poured a generous amount of whiskey from a cut-glass
decanter into a tumbler, George stared at her. The sleeveless, white
velvet gown clung to her shape, revealing her small waist. Her high-
boned cheeks were pale, her eyes clear and shining. About the only
color on her face was that of her lipstick, a deep red. She had brushed
her hair into a loose chignon, fastening it at the nape of her neck with
a comb of some sort. Shaped like a leaf, it was studded with diamonds.

"Let's go to the patio in the back. The night is so lovely."

A few minutes later the couple sat down on a rattan, padded
couch. George, taking in the grandeur around him, put his arm around
Lenora and moved to kiss her. "What a perfect setting for our first
night together in this place," he said, as he ran his fingers along her
neck. "This house is a dream."

"George," Lenora began, "I don't think we have ever talked about your visit to the island. That first visit. What did you do? Where did you go?"

"About a year before I met you," and he paused to kiss her on the cheek, "I was at an air race in Chicago. I met a flyer there from Florida. I think he was from Miami. Anyway, the two of us got to talking about the most beautiful spots we had visited, and he kept telling me I had to come."

"And?"

"Well, I traveled mostly near San Juan. But first I went to the rain forest. I'll never forget the flock of wild parrots I saw; they were magnificent. As far as the towns were concerned, well, I'd have to say the poverty troubled me. I know I keep repeating myself, but how do most of the people get by?"

"Many of them don't. That is the problem. I could talk about their plight for hours, really. But, now, I'd rather hear more about you."

"Well, I am famished," said George. "How about some chow."

After they had eaten their meal, George brought a bottle of champagne into the parlor and sat down beside Lenora. Taking a sip of the cool, fizzy wine, he closed his eyes and put his head on her lap. Lenora flipped off her shoes and, raising her legs to the couch, bent down and kissed his forehead.

As she sipped from her glass, George put a small red box, which he had tucked away inside his jacket pocket, on his chest for her to see. "Merry Christmas, sweetheart."

"I have something for you, but I'll have to get up."

"No, no. Stay as you are." Then, he brought her flushed face close to his.

WONDERMENT

$\mathcal{P}$etrona was making breakfast in the early hours of the morning. The arousing, distinctive aromas of cinnamon rolls in the oven, sausage frying, rich Puerto Rican coffee on the stove stirred George awake from, what was for him, an unusually sound sleep.

For a while, he stared above him at the eyelet canopy of his four-poster bed. The matress was firm, the sheets, silken soft. He could hear the lulling pull of waves from the open window. Sunlight poured into the room and danced along the unadorned white walls. The place was extraordinarily tranquil. So removed from the rushed, mechanical life that was his in America.

Could Lenora really leave this house and setting? And even if she did, could she forget this existence to which she was obviously attached. Apparently, from what he could see, she had created a world for herself in Puerto Rico. She seemed very much at home.

He got up from his bed, ducking underneath the netting meant to keep away mosquitoes and all manner of other unappealing insects, and paced the length of the room. Taking an orange, he began to peel away the rind. He wondered whether it would be possible for him to leave his school behind in Hempstead to live on the island with her.

From the window came the sounds of hammering and men's loud voices yelling and laughing. Wiping sticky juice from his chin with a handkerchief, he looked out to see twenty or more laborers, dressed in overalls and short-sleeved shirts, dragging long planks to an area not too far from the patio. Some were carrying bundles of rope, and others, large palm fronds. He decided to join them.

But before getting dressed he walked over to a large oak chest and picked up the beautiful wood-framed photograph, Lenora's Christmas gift to him. He looked closely at the picture. Never had he thought that so many tonalities of gray, black, and white could be assigned to a photographic print. He had never heard of Alfred Stieglitz, but he certainly had captured the essence of the New York landscape George knew well. The photograph was alive in its conveyance of primeval glory. It was a simple study, and yet complex. A few large chestnut trees in a field. The trees looked like satiny sculpture. The field, a golden, glittering constellation.

But no matter how much he might appreciate the artistry of the picture, he wondered why Lenora had not chosen to give him something more personal—a photo of herself, perhaps.

WOMAN TO WOMAN

Upon awaking that last day in December, Lenora sat up in bed and reached for the gift that George had given her the night before.

Opening the small velvet box, she looked inside once more. As she admired the beautiful earrings, she thought about what George had said upon presenting them to her. "I've often wondered about the blue necklace that you wear. I asked my aunt about it, and she told me the stones were aquamarine—*'A coincidence, George, because I have a very lovely pair of earrings in the shop that would match her necklace perfectly. Italian. Would you like to see?'*—Well, I hope you like them, Lenora."

They were, quite remarkably, a perfect match for her favorite necklace. She put the earrings on, got up from bed, and walked to her vanity. Yes, they were the ideal size, discreet. Framed in ornate gold work, they dropped just below the earlobe.

She opened the drawer to her vanity, pulled out a packet of envelopes, and found the letter that Janet had sent to her just a few months before. "Dearest Lenora," it began, "I hope this letter finds you well. I've been thinking about you often these days." Somewhat abruptly it continued. "Please dear, forgive my imprudence, for I know that it is terribly unwise to interfere in someone's romance, particularly when it concerns a favorite nephew. I suppose it is my love for George—he is like a son to me—that allows me to throw caution to the wind in this instance. Anyway, I felt that I should tell you that my nephew is completely devoted to you. His is a very strong affection. He talks of nothing but marrying Lenora Demarest and... how you both could start an aviation company together in New York. He has very clear plans. I do worry, though. I wonder, is this something you wish for, too? Please know that, while George Hanson doesn't look it—the athletic physique, cavalier air—he is, deep down, quite vulnerable. Very tender, indeed. Well, I have surely said too much already, but I did think that "a little bird" ought to carry this message, woman to woman. Stay well, dear. Affectionately, Janet."

When Lenora had first read the letter she had to admit she was somewhat annoyed, for this was interference of a most forward kind. But after she had given the matter more thought, she realized Janet had taken a calculated risk, that she had meant no harm at all; rather the opposite. For if not Janet, who else to speak the truth? And the truth was that Lenora really did not want to change her life. She was perfectly happy with things as they were.

She quickly dressed, looked out the window at the activity below, and hurried to the kitchen for her morning cup of *café con leche*.

THE PARTY

That night, at eight o' clock, the workers of La Sardinera plantation—pickers, packers, field hands, and carpenters—started arriving at the house. The men were decked out in their finest suits of cream-and-white-colored linen and heavy cotton, the women in their prettiest dancing dresses with blossoms in their hair.

Earlier that day, George had helped erect the picnic tables, wide wood planks placed on trestles—twenty in all. Empty rum casks served as chairs. With Petrona's help, Lenora had strung line after line of Chinese tasseled lanterns between the royal palms around the house.

Looking down at the yard from her bedroom window, she admired the scene. A simple presentation of picnic tables covered in white crepe paper, softly glowing pale red illuminations swinging in the breeze. Lenora watched as Petrona greeted the guests. What would she have done without this competent, amiable woman? She noticed that Pepe and Marianela were walking arm and arm toward the beach. They stopped just short of where Rosita had been found that awful November afternoon four years earlier. Crossing themselves, they abruptly turned around and headed back to the growing group of revelers.

Dressed only in a lacy slip, Lenora slowly walked around her bedroom, wondering what to wear that evening. Something festive, yet not too fancy. She opened the ornately carved mahogany armoire and stared inside, first taking out a simple lavender ensemble of jacket and long skirt then putting it back in favor of an orange crepe silk robe, with a light green, silver-threaded sash, loose-fitting sleeves. Kimono style.

Slipping into the comfortable dress—it was so cool and soft upon her skin—she quickly tied the sash around her waist and looked into the floor-length mirror. With a pair of silver high-heeled slippers, it was perfect.

She tied her hair into a knot, put on the aquamarine earrings. A touch of pomegranate-tinted lipstick, a pat of rouge. A splash of Agua de Sevilla. She was ready.

She walked down the staircase to the candle-lit parlor. As she entered, George let out a whistle. "Beautiful. You look beautiful, darling. Then with great fanfare, he poured two shots of rum and handed one to her. "To the future. Our future."

Later, after everyone had eaten heaping plates of delectable food—pots and pots of rice and herb-flavored red beans, whipped yams flavored with carmelized brown sugar, cinnamon, and cumin, enormous platters of crispy roast pork, fried crab, and chicken *asopao*—the merriment began.

At first, just a few enthusiastic couples got up on the dance floor. But, gradually, as the music became heated with African rhythms, more people were moving their feet, shoulders, and hips to the lively, intoxicating beat of *güiro*, maracas, and guitar.

George, who had never danced to music of this kind, watched some of the men out of the corner of his eye. They were drenched with sweat, eyes closed, and moving gracefully to the rapid-fire *plena*. He felt embarrassed by his awkward movements. Drawing back, he held Lenora's hand. "Hey, darling, I can't compete with these guys." But when the band played a tango, Lenora led George out to the center of the group. "I've never danced the tango in my life. And I know that you haven't. But, heck, this is New Year's Eve."

She knew that he was enjoying the moment just as much as she, savoring the atmosphere of the balmy evening, under a sky streaked here and there with gauzy cloud, the ocean swoosh just behind them, and the sweet perfume of flora.

Just before midnight, Lenora gave George a passionate kiss, excused herself, and quickly walked toward a shaded area near the beach. Finding the men whom she had hired to create the firework extravaganza, she checked to make certain that everything was ready to begin upon the last toll, the twelfth, of the large bell at the house. Pepe had volunteered to do the honors.

Rushing back to her guests, she asked Petrona's nieces to begin uncorking the champagne. Then, she signaled to the band to stop the music.

The bell began to toll, once, twice, thrice, and on and on, until the last toll echoed to a vibrating silence. A distant rushing, like a stormy wind, announced the first of many Roman candles speeding toward the height of darkness, showering the night with green and pink, red and gold confetti lights. A sharp whistle. A burst of fiery blue sunflowers, petals breaking off and falling ever slowly, disappearing. High-pitched strains announced three pinwheels turning light and trailing tendrons of vermilion. Next a popping, funneling of rays, first purple, then red, and orange interceded by the zigzagging of silvery tassels exploding into golden snowflakes.

George, putting his hand on the small of her back, led Lenora away from the others.

"Darling, where can we go to talk. Someplace quiet."

"Back to the house," she answered, as she put her arm around his waist. "The second-floor terrace?"

As the couple ascended the staircase Lenora was preparing herself for the conversation she had known would come that evening. She began to organize her thoughts, running through the many explanations, reasons, answers she had committed to memory in anticipation of this moment.

From the terrace, they looked down at the revelers. The music had begun again, and everyone was dancing, swaying to the cadence of the New Year cycle, the unstoppable passing of seconds and minutes that would turn into hours, days, and months, the forward thrust of time that led to loss of time, the impossible command of the present.

"Lenora, darling," whispered George, as he wrapped his arms around her waist, "we haven't talked about our wedding once since I have come. Why is that?"

Looking past his shoulder, toward the spray of pompom fireworks, she remembered something he had written to her. How had he put it? *"The atmosphere above us is rare, complex. Of several distinct and purposeful parts. A blinding place of stars and cosmic rays. Sometimes when I ponder the infinity of space, I shudder."*

The mystery of it all. Of wanting and not having, of hoping and yearning, of needing, always needing more and more. When did desire end? What was the ancient Greek adage? Was it Pliny the Younger who said, "An object in possession seldom retains the same charm it had in pursuit."

The stars were so bright, the moon was a cut-away sliver. How pleasing to the soul, how very perfect was the fullness of silence.

THE TRUTH

 aving said good night to Lenora rather huffily—as she had stood on the terrace calling after him, "Please, George, oh, come back"—he tore off to his room and slammed the door shut, kicking at it more than once.

He poured a glass of water, took off his jacket, and rolled up the sleeves of his shirt. So agitated and offended was he that he could not stop moving about, occasionally hitting the walls with his left fist. Finally, concentrating on the room in which he found himself alone on such a festive night, he opened the window as wide as possible. Straddling a chair, and resting his arms on its back, he inhaled the cool, salty air in measured breaths. Confused, he looked out at the dancers, everyone so happy and carefree. What, my God, had happened just moments ago? He almost thought he might have understood if Lenora had said, "There is someone else, George." Although having to hear such a confession, he supposed, would not be any easier on him.

He gulped down his water and poured another glass.

Well, now, she had played with him, in a way. For chrissake, why had she invited him to Puerto Rico for this—this slap in the face? He hadn't thought she had a cruel bone in her body.

He thought about her explanation and tried to find a clue as to what was going on with her.

"I do love you, George, you know that, darling. But I also love aviation—I think I have a future in flying, not just flying for fun but helping to advance the place of women in the industry; you were the one who helped me understand that there is so much we women fly-ers can do. And I have my work on the farm. I don't think that I could ever leave this place. As I see it, the problem is this: if we marry, well, eventually, maybe not right away, but sooner or later, you will coax me toward domestic concerns, wifely obligations that will, no doubt, prevent me from giving as much time as I want to my own pursuits. I don't think that I can ever be Mrs. George Hanson. I would not know who that is. But I always will be Lenora Demarest in love with George Hanson."

The aviator got up from his chair and rubbed his eyes. Had it really taken this, the ultimate step in their courtship, to make him see that he had, quite simply, met his match? He grinned. *She would not submit.* He hadn't thought of that before.

EPILOGUE

AUTUMN 1938

$\mathcal{I}$t was blinding, so affirming was the sunlight that as she flew toward Cuba she wondered if she would recognize the island's mass. Sea and earth were nearly indistinguishable in such brightness.

Imagining the course ahead, she could feel her pulse racing. Although a little nervous, she was thrilled by the prospect of flying for the first time ever to Chautauqua. She had been dreaming about this Atlantic flight for so many years; now she was undertaking it in memory of Amelia.

Amelia, dearest friend, she mused, whatever happened? You who so abhorred the confinement of marriage and yet married; you who were so prepared and yet so care-less on your most perilous journey.

She had been extremely pleased that Amelia had accepted her invitation to spend the night in Puerto Rico on her first stop around the globe. *Had it really been just one year ago?* But when she sensed Amelia's insouciant mood that evening at La Sardinera, she had felt alarmed by what she perceived to be a hastily planned trip, and she had sought to dissuade her friend from making the high-speed celes-

233

tial flight. Perhaps if Amelia had been willing to linger over dinner and the conversation hadn't seemed so polite, what with Fred Noonan listening in, she might have been able to convince her friend that the journey was, at the very least, ill-advised. Especially at that time of the year with less than perfect weather conditions. And going east around the equator? What had alarmed her even more was Amelia's admission that neither she nor Noonan knew Morse code. "Amelia," Lenora had asked, "how on earth do you think you'll find this Howland Island, which is minuscule, a mile long you say, without emergency tools. It seems foolhardy." And Amelia's incredible response, while laughing. "Don't fret so. Jackie Cochran told me that if something happens, she'll find us using extrasensory perception. She really is remarkably gifted." And then, Fred had quipped, with a silly grin, "Hey, don't forget that I'm a damn good navigator."

Now, reading her compass, she saw that she was close to Havana's coast and began her descent. Turning west, she sped through a wall of white, keeping calm through the turbulence, staying vigilant. As *The Flamboyant* finally broke free, she saw the outline of the island, making out a silvery sand belt against roiling indigo. Keep steady, she thought. She remembered what a pilot once told her about the waters off Havana. "Shark-infested, so shark-infested that you never want to even think about the possibility of a sea landing."

She sped over the magnificent Morro fortress. There. The airstrip was just ahead. Squinting through her goggles, she could see it clearly.

She had never been to Havana; perhaps she should spend the night, take a look around, and see a show or two. She really wasn't in a hurry. She could make her hops quite leisurely toward New York City and then on to Chautauqua. Amelia had told her that the leg from San Juan to Miami was "a friendly course." So she could spare a few days. If her calculations were correct the autumn leaves would peak in a few weeks' time. And maybe, she certainly was hoping, she would be able to convince George to fly out and join her for a few days of rest at Driftwood.

FALL 1991

San Juan Star, October 18, 1991

LENORA DEMAREST, PUERTO RICO'S
FIRST AVIATRIX, DEAD AT 91

Lenora Demarest, longtime resident of Dorado, Puerto Rico, died on October 15 in Jamestown, New York. She was Puerto Rico's first aviatrix and devoted much of her life to the Civil Air Patrol, holding both the deputy commander and commander CAP positions.

The ninety-one-year-old suffered a stroke at her Chautauqua Lake estate, which she called Driftwood. Trapped alone inside her home, she survived for six days without food or water. After being found, she was taken to the Women's Christian Association Hospital in Jamestown, New York, where she later died of congestive heart failure.

Demarest was brought to Puerto Rico in 1917 by her father, Dr. Henry Demarest, a widower. The family owned a grapefruit plantation at La Sardinera, the site where a luxury hotel now stands.

After her father's death in the 1920s, Lenora Demarest ran the grapefruit farm until its sale to a prominent New York businessman in 1958. As part of the deal, she was given twenty acres and a house for life. She left Puerto Rico in 1980.

When Amelia Earhart made her fateful flight in 1937, she and her navigator, Fred Noonan, made their first stop in Puerto Rico and spent the night at Lenora Demarest's estate, known as La Sardinera.

As the two hundredth licensed woman pilot in the United States, Demarest also became America's eleventh licensed helicopter pilot. She was a flight instructor in the U.S. Army Air Corps.

In the 1930s Lenora Demarest opened a flying school in Puerto Rico that evolved into a coed youth training program with three thousand members, thirteen to twenty years old. During the Second World War she engaged in dangerous search-and-rescue missions, among them one in which she was able to locate a sinking barge in Lake Erie in near zero visibility. She was also a courier, flying planes across the continent.

In addition to running a successful export business and supporting various Puerto Rican charities, she felt her greatest accomplishment was "when I gave fifty acres of land to the forty families who worked La Sardinera and helped to make my business successful. I feel enormous satisfaction when I think that these people, who had never owned property before, finally had land of their own."

ACKNOWLEDGMENTS

Heartfelt thanks to my editor, Julia Serebrinsky, and Jennifer Lyons, as well as to the individuals at HarperCollins who have been involved in the publication of my novel. To the congenial staff of the Hyatt Dorado Beach Hotel, I extend my appreciation for the courtesy shown to me during my visit in January 2001. While researching the subject of early aviation, several books were helpful, particularly *Women Aloft* by Valerie Moolman, *Sisters of the Wind* by Elizabeth S. Bell, and *The Stars at Noon* by Jacqueline Cochran. This is a work of fiction, and as such, the descriptions of my characters and their actions are drawn from my imagination, but my portrait of Lenora Demarest was inspired, in part, by the American aviatrix Clara Livingston, who came to my attention by way of an article in the *Jamestown Post-Journal*. The poem, *El Flamboyán*, which I have translated on page 210 is by the Puerto Rican poet José Augustín Balseiro Ramos. Flamenco lyrics on pages 163–65 are traditional; translations are mine.